# BOOTS & LEATHER

## UGLY STICK SALOON BOOK #3

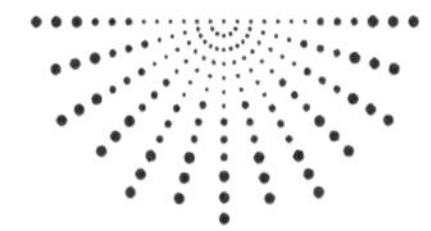

## MYLA JACKSON

TWISTED PAGE INC

# BOOTS & LEATHER

## UGLY STICK SALOON BOOK #3

*New York Times* & *USA Today*
Bestselling Author

ELLE JAMES

*writing as*

MYLA JACKSON

EBOOK ISBN: 978-1-62695-092-4

PRINTISBN: 978-1-62695-094-8

*This book is dedicated people who know what they want
and go after it until they finally succeed.*

*She's a free-riding, biker-chick with attitude...they're just the Kiowa cowboys who can rein her in.*

Libby Jones had been on the road for over a year, running from her past, when she lands in Temptation, Texas, working at the Ugly Stick Saloon. Eight months later, she knows she must leave or risk her past catching up with her. Then why did she take the Gray Wolf twins up on an offer to go riding on their ranch? Getting involved isn't in the cards for this free-rider.

Mark and Luke Gray Wolf have been trying to capture Libby Jones's attention since she'd started work at the Ugly Stick, only she's blown them off at every attempt to ask her out, until now. Determined to show her a good time on the ranch, they take her to their special project site and show her what she's been missing. Their plan: to expose her to the temptations only twins can provide to persuade her to stay for the long haul.

Convinced she's falling for the two, Libby longs for a life she can't have, knowing she must leave before her whereabouts are discovered. But all hell breaks loose when her past walks through the doors of the saloon. The Gray Wolf twins have a fight on their hands to keep Libby from running again.

**Warning:** This title contains hot scenes with even hotter Kiowa twins and a motorcyle-riding, leather-clad biker chick. Caution—bring your fan and iced drinks to the reading, the pages sizzle!

# AUTHOR'S NOTE

Enjoy other Ugly Stick Saloon books by Myla Jackson

***Ugly Stick Saloon Series***

Boots & Chaps (#1)

Boots & Sex Ed (#2)

Boots & Leather (#3)

Boots & Promises (#4)

Boots & Bareback (#5)

Boots & Dirty Tricks (#6)

Boots & Lace (#7)

Boots & Roses (#8)

Boots & Buckles (#9)

Boots & the Wishes (#10)

Boots & Twisters (#11)

Boots & the Bachelor (#12)

Boots & The Rogue (#13)

Boots & The Heartbreaker (#14)

Boots & Wings (#15)

Visit Mylajackson.com for more information

Visit her alter ego Elle James at ellejames.com

Join Elle James and Myla Jackson's Newsletter at

http://ellejames.com/ElleContact.htm

*L*ibby Jones flipped the whiskey bottle in the air and caught it without spilling a drop, then poured a round of shots for the two men who'd pulled up stools at the bar. She filled two mugs with beer from the tap and slapped them on the counter. "Anything else I can do for you boys?"

"How's about a lap dance, beautiful?" one suggested, grinning. His smile displayed two missing front teeth.

The man beside him elbowed him in the gut. "What would yer wife say, Harmon?"

Harmon shrugged. "She'd probably tell me to take out the trash."

"Yeah, meaning you. Then she'd knock the rest of those teeth out of that stupid head of yers."

"Shut up, Reggie." Harmon frowned. "Got those teeth knocked out ridin' a bull on the circuit."

"That bull bein' the husband of that ugly redhead

in Amarillo." Reggie slapped a hand on Harmon's back and roared with laughter. "Wasn't worth it, was it?"

Libby sighed. The same old drunks with the same stories always managed to end up at her barstools. Where were all the good-looking cowboys tonight? She glanced across the crowded saloon. That's where they were. On the dance floor, while she was serving drinks behind the bar.

The Gray Wolf twins, Mark and Luke, spun around for the umpteenth time, laughing and smiling, making every girl in the place drool.

*Even me.* Libby sighed again. Back in her other life, she'd be the one dancing and someone else would be serving her drinks. But then, she'd hated her other life. No. Libby was better off tending bar and keeping to herself than playing the pampered princess in a city full of people. At least in Temptation, Texas, she could get away from the noise and crowds when she wanted.

Audrey Anderson, the owner of the Ugly Stick Saloon, laid a hand on Libby's shoulder. "'Bout ready for your break?"

"Past ready." Libby pulled the towel off her shoulder and tossed it on the bar. "I'll be out back."

"The cowboys 'round here can get pretty rowdy," Audrey warned. "You sure you'll be all right?"

"Better than being inside all night." Libby burst through the back door of the saloon into the night, sucking in a deep breath of fresh air that didn't reek of alcohol and sweaty men.

Eight months she'd been working at the Ugly Stick

Saloon. Longer than anywhere else she'd stayed over the past couple years. Eight months she'd been watching others having fun and partying, flirting with the handsome cowboys, two of whom had definitely caught her eye since she'd started working at the saloon. Libby's shoulders tensed. She was better off forgetting about flirting with the Gray Wolf men. A low profile had been her goal for the past two years and the only thing that kept her out of trouble.

Still, she had yearnings...needs...a hunger for something more.

Perhaps it was time to move on.

The door behind her opened and closed, footsteps crunching in the gravel toward her.

She walked faster, craving the quiet time alone. Before she'd gone two yards, the footsteps caught up with her and hands slid down her shoulders.

"Hey, beautiful. Need a ride home?" A big, smelly man with bad breath and shaggy hair spun her around.

"No. I don't need a ride." She tried to shake his hands off, but they were like meaty vise grips, clamped down hard enough to leave bruises.

A spike of adrenaline zipped through her bloodstream as the heat of anger built. She hated being held against her will. For the past two years, she'd lived free of constraint of any kind. She'd be damned if any man would hold her back again. "Let go of me before I hurt you."

The man guffawed, spewing clouds of alcohol vapor in her face. "A little thang like you? Hurt me?"

She raised her knee in a quick jerk, connecting with the drunk's private parts.

The foul-mouthed man let go of her arms and grabbed his crotch, swearing in a high-pitched whine. "Damn, girl, I'll get ya for that."

"Yeah, right. Go home to your wife and sleep it off." She backed away and walked on, dogged by the sound of multiple footsteps in the gravel now following her. When she reached a row of cars, she stopped and wheeled around to face the new threat. "What do you want?"

The two men who looked remarkably alike and dressed identically in crisp white button-down dress shirts and neatly pressed jeans, stood in front of her, hands raised in surrender and grinning. Libby's heartbeat ratcheted up a notch as she stared at the Gray Wolf twins. The men she'd been drooling over not five minutes earlier.

"Audrey sent us out here to keep an eye on her favorite bartender," one of them said.

The other's eyes twinkled. "Seems like you can take care of yourself pretty well on your own. Ol' Pleaze won't try messing with you again."

If Libby had been wondering where all the good-looking cowboys had gone, she'd found the two most qualified. "Jackpot," she said beneath her breath.

The Gray Wolf brothers had to be the best-looking cowboys in the area, especially the twins. Their dark-skin, long, pitch-black hair and brown-black eyes spoke of their Kiowa Indian roots and had every girl this side of the Brazos River panting.

Libby had to admit, she'd panted a time or two over them from behind the bar. More and more lately. They'd made an effort to stop by and talk to her whenever she had a free moment, not that she encouraged them. It was nice on the ego to know she still had it, and appealed to a couple of damned good-looking men. Not that she could take advantage of it and flirt back. Relationships weren't in the cards for her. The twins had impeccable reputations as gentlemen and cowboys. Where women were concerned, the Gray Wolfs made fine catches.

She'd come outside for freedom from noise and people, not to start up a conversation with the cowboys. "I don't need a babysitter, but thanks anyway."

She turned and walked farther away from the building, until the thump, thump, thump of the music blaring inside the corrugated tin walls subsided some.

The crunch of boots on the gravel indicated her tails hadn't taken the hint.

"Shh!" She faced the men and pressed a finger to her lips. "Hear that?"

Both men shook their heads, the similarity between the twins so remarkable, Libby had never been able to tell them apart by looks, only by personality.

Mark, the fun-loving, more outgoing one of the pair grinned. "I don't hear a thing."

Luke shook his head. "That's her point, brother. She came out for quiet, not to hear us flapping our jaws. Come on." Luke grabbed his brother's arm. "Leave Libby alone."

"No, I'm here to watch out for the pretty lady," Mark insisted. "I don't shirk my responsibility."

"You heard her. She can take care of herself." Luke snorted. "You just wanna flirt."

"Damn right." Mark grabbed Libby's hand, swung her out and back in with his best dance move. When he had her in the crook of his arm, he whispered, "I've been trying to get inside your panties since you started here at the Ugly Stick."

Libby's pussy clenched at the thought of Mark in her panties, but she pushed the image aside and twirled out, putting distance between her and Mark. "You and every other horndog in this joint."

"Smooth, dickhead. I'm sure she goes for those kinds of come-ons." Luke reached out and captured Libby's hand. "Excuse my coarse brother, he never learned manners."

Libby laughed. Mark and Luke always had a way of lightening her dark thoughts. "You two are too much. How come you haven't found girlfriends?"

Mark grinned. "We've been waiting for you, darlin'." He took her hand again and brought it to his lips.

Luke squeezed the fingers on her other hand gently, his gaze capturing hers, dark and intense. "We were meant for the forever kind of love, not just flirting."

Luke's words made the smile slip from Libby's lips, the hands holding hers suddenly feeling like manacles. She tugged loose and stepped back, the trapped feeling making her chest tighten, her breaths shorten and her feet itch to run.

"See there, Luke. You're scaring her now." Mark rolled his eyes. "Can't decide if the bullshit is on the inside or the outside of his boots."

Libby pulled away, fighting to breathe past the lump forming in her throat. When she spied her black and red Harley Davidson motorcycle, she hurried toward it, the road calling to her. Not until she'd swung her leg over the seat and braced her hands on the grips did she feel reason return and with it, the confirmation it was time to move on.

The twins followed, staying true to their promise to Audrey to look out for Libby.

"Beautiful." Luke smoothed his hand along the white angel wings painted across the black gas tank, but his eyes were on Libby, not the wings. "There's nothing like riding, is there?"

"Nothing," she agreed, her gaze captured by his intensely dark and sincere eyes.

These men weren't just about flirting and scoring with every woman they met. They'd proven over and over that they were honest, helpful and kind as well. On more than one occasion, they'd lent their construction experience to Audrey and the Ugly Stick, free of charge. As Libby knew, not every handsome man had that kind of integrity. Libby had met her share of horses' asses back in New York City. She suspected the oldest of the Gray Wolf brothers, Jackson, had a lot to do with Mark and Luke's good manners, having raised them since their parents died.

"I've always imagined riding a bike is like riding a horse," Luke continued.

"It's better." Libby tipped her head back in an attempt to ignore the twinkle in his eyes. "It's like pure freedom."

"You seem to know your way around a motorcycle." Mark touched the leather seat. "Have you always been a biker?"

Libby's lips quirked and she opened her eyes. "No. Not always."

"Then why biking?" he asked.

"I go where and when I want to." Libby tipped her chin up as a light breeze lifted the hair off her neck. "No strings, no holds, just me and the road."

"That's how I feel when I'm on horseback." Luke glanced down at the bike.

"Have you ever ridden a horse?" Mark asked.

She nodded. "Lots of times."

Mark's brows rose. "Really? Around here?"

"No," she answered. "Back in New York City." As soon as the words were out of her mouth, Libby regretted them. The less anyone knew about her former life, the better.

Mark snorted. "That's not riding, that's walking the dog. I'm talking about really riding across the range, over acres and acres, with the sun on your back and nothing around but the horse and the sky." He patted his chest. "Now that's freedom."

Libby tilted her head. She'd never seen Mark so

quietly enthused. Most often he was raising a ruckus on the dance floor, twirling some pretty young thing in a short, flouncy skirt and studded cowboy boots. When he talked about riding, his face grew serious, his expression dreamy and far away.

God, he was gorgeous. Libby's tummy tightened. "No, I haven't ridden like that." But the way he talked about it made her want to.

"You should come with us," Luke said. "Why not Thursday? You're usually off on Thursday, aren't you?"

Libby frowned, not sure whether she should be annoyed or flattered that Luke knew so much about her work schedule. For certain, she didn't like the way her pulse sped at the thought of spending the day with the Gray Wolf men.

"I have…plans."

"Can't you change them?" Mark asked. "We can show you the ranch. The weather's supposed to be warm and sunny, not too hot."

The tug of the road pulled at Libby. With a man on either side of her, she felt just a little hemmed in… trapped. She got off her bike and stepped out of their overpowering huddle.

"No…no, I can't change my plans." Agreeing to go out with the men would be the biggest commitment she'd made in the past eight months, second only to hiring on at the Ugly Stick Saloon and becoming fast friends with her boss.

"What plans?" Mark demanded, coming after her.

She backed up another step, her gaze going to

Luke who'd stood back, his brows dipping slightly. "I don't know…plans." Heat rose up her neck, spreading out into her cheeks at the lie.

"Back off, Mark. You're crowding her." Luke grabbed his brother's arm and held him steady while Libby stepped farther away.

Mark shook off Luke's hand and stood still, letting the gap between himself and Libby widen. "You like peace and quiet don't you?" he asked, his tone softer, gentler, his eyes wide like a sad puppy's, begging for affection. Beautiful and dangerous to her control.

Libby couldn't resist, and nodded. "Yes."

"And she's not getting much of that now." Luke shook his head. "Look, if you feel like getting out in the open air, no cars, no honking, nobody to pester you but the two of us—and I promise we won't pester you too much—drop by our place at eleven o'clock on Thursday. We'd love for you to join us on a ride."

Libby's eyes narrowed. The way Luke had pulled his brother back and left the invitation open appealed to her, making her wonder what it would be like to have more of his intuitive attention, maybe even having those large, capable hands skimming across her skin, awakening places that had been long dormant. And Mark's broad shoulders and eager, brown-eyed gaze tripped her heartbeat and sent butterflies fluttering through her belly. No. She shook her head in an attempt to clear it of the vision of delicious twin cowboys. She couldn't get sucked in. She opened her mouth to decline.

Luke put up a hand. "Don't decide now. Sleep on it. You have a couple days to think about it."

"We can be as peaceful and quiet as you want," Mark promised.

Libby couldn't help her snort. "Mark…quiet? I don't think I've ever seen you quiet."

His brows furrowed. "I can be, especially out on the ranch."

She sighed. "I'll think about it."

"Great!" Mark clapped his hands together. "We'll see you at eleven on Thursday. Wear boots and jeans. We'll make it a picnic."

Libby chuckled. "I said I'd think about it."

"Libby!" Audrey's voice carried across the back parking lot.

"We'll be countin' the minutes until we see you again." Luke captured her hand and lifted it to his lips.

Libby's cheeks warmed and a deep yearning low in her belly blossomed, making her ache for more than just a kiss on her hand.

"The two of us will make it a treat you won't forget," Mark promised, sweeping her into a bear hug, lifting her off the ground and planting a kiss on her surprised lips. Before she could find her wits to struggle, he set her back on her feet and tucked something in her jeans' pocket. "If you need us for anything…" He waggled his eyebrows. "And I mean anything… call." He spun her toward the building and patted her bottom.

Libby hurried back into the saloon, wondering what had just happened. She pulled a card from her hip pocket and stared down at the logo for Gray Wolf Architectural Designs and the phone number listed.

"Oh good, I was beginning to think the twins had absconded with my best bartender." Audrey leaned closer, her eyes narrowing. "Are you all right?"

Libby jammed the card back into her pocket, frowning. "I think I'm going on a picnic."

Audrey laughed. "Did Mark and Luke talk you into an outing?" She patted Libby on the back. "Babe, you're in for a real treat."

"That's what *they* said." A tingle of excitement threatened to grow inside Libby's body.

A secret smile lifted Audrey's lips. "The two of them are amazing together."

Her frown deepening, Libby glanced across at her boss. "And you know that *how?*"

Audrey's lips quirked upward in a smirk. "Did I tell you the story of how they got me and Jackson together?" She slipped her arm around Libby's shoulder and walked her slowly into the bar.

"No, you didn't."

Audrey touched a finger to her own lips. "Hmm. Maybe I shouldn't, and let you discover for yourself why those two are phenomenal."

Libby's core tightened, a wash of moisture trickling out of what she'd thought was her dried-up pussy, shocking her more than she cared to admit. She marched the rest of the way to the bar and took up her bar towel. "I've a good mind to cancel."

"No way," Audrey called out.

Her heart sped and pressure pushed against her

chest, the sure signs of the beginnings of an anxiety attack.

Audrey laid a hand on her arm. "You have to go on that picnic. I promise you won't regret it."

Forcing a smile for the next customer, Libby muttered beneath her breath, "I think I already am." *Yeah, yeah.* Then why did a shiver of anticipation spread throughout her body?

# CHAPTER TWO

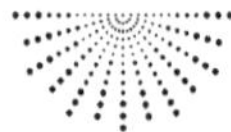

*B*y the time the saloon closed, Libby could barely think of anything else...and the *date* was two days away. She finished cleaning up the bar and called out a goodbye as she passed the storeroom.

Audrey echoed her good night and giggled. The low rumble of a male voice sounded behind the door.

Squelching the urge to peek into the storeroom, Libby sailed by, knowing Jackson Gray Wolf had her boss cornered, probably doing naughty things to her among the stacks of supplies.

With a sigh, Libby let herself out the back door of the saloon and strode toward the spot she'd left her motorcycle. How long had it been since she'd had sex? Too damn long. The invitation from Mark and Luke had been the first time she'd been tempted. The riding date was two days away, making her *dry spell* that much longer.

She passed by Audrey's red pickup and Jackson's black one and ground to a stop, shock stealing her breath away. Her precious motorcycle lay on the ground, the leather seat slashed, a mirror broken and the acrid stench of gasoline filling the air.

"Damn!" Anger shot through her veins as she closed the distance, inspecting the damage. Someone had deliberately sabotaged her bike, tipping over *The Beast.*

Libby struggled to right the machine, fury giving her the strength to set it on its wheels despite the weight. Once she had it upright, she straddled the seat and flicked the starter. The engine turned over once and then nothing. She tried several more times, still nothing.

With a sigh, she hung her head, tired and a little defeated. Then she noticed the large damp spot on the gravel where the gasoline had spilled. She checked the fuel gauge and groaned.

She'd had just enough to get her home and to the station the next day. Now, the tank was completely empty. And she had no idea if anything else had been tampered with. No doubt a disgruntled customer or that man she'd kneed in the groin had done this, knowing exactly who the bike belonged to. Not until the following morning, when the garage that serviced her bike opened, would she know the full extent of damage to her *baby.*

She patted the tank like a favored child. "Don't you worry, Beast. We'll have you fixed up in no time."

With no other alternatives, Libby trudged back

into the saloon. Everyone else had gone except Audrey and Jackson. From the noise on the other side of the storeroom door, they were getting it on. At least someone was having some fun.

Reluctant to disturb the private party, Libby wandered around to the bar and sat at one of the stools, prepared to wait them out. After ten minutes, Audrey and Jackson still hadn't emerged and Libby was getting tired of waiting. The waitresses had gone earlier, before Libby had finished cleaning and restocking the bar. They were probably sleeping soundly by now, their aching feet propped up in bed.

Libby wiggled her toes in her black leather boots. What she wouldn't give for a long, hot shower, or better yet, a steaming bubble bath. Had she been in New York City, she'd have called a cab. No such convenience existed in the counties on either side of the Ugly Stick Saloon. If you needed a ride, you called a friend.

As that thought passed through her mind, Libby remembered the card in her back pocket. Mark and Luke had said if she needed them, just call.

She pulled the card from her pocket and stared down at the stiff paper with the bold print. Her head tipped toward the storeroom, where giggles and noises indicated no end to their antics anytime soon.

She slipped her cell phone from her purse, studying the display screen, stalling. For once she had three bars service. At the Ugly Stick, reception was always questionable. Maybe it was a sign. Quickly, before she could change her mind, she dialed the number on the card, half-hoping the men wouldn't answer.

After only one ring, a deep male voice cut through the line. "Libby?

For a moment, her voice froze, and the hand holding the phone shook.

"Libby? Are you there? Tell me this isn't a butt-dial." A deep chuckle rumbled in her ear.

"No butt-dial. I'm here." A smile tugged at her lips and she relaxed a little. "Which one of you did I get?"

"This is Luke. Are you all right?"

Warmth filled the empty spot in her chest at the sound of concern in Luke's voice. How could she let herself get so needy? When she'd left home, she'd vowed to be independent no matter what. Regretting the call already, she almost hung up, but knew it would be rude. "I'm sorry, I shouldn't have called. You two are probably in bed already."

"No, no. We're glad you called. And we haven't even started home yet. We're over at the truck stop in Temptation, finishing an early breakfast. Wanna join us?"

"No. Thanks." She shifted her hand, ready to click the off button at the soonest possible chance.

"Where are you?" Luke asked, forestalling her sudden urge to end the conversation.

She breathed a long, deep sigh and went with the flow. Hell, she'd already called, she might as well ask for a ride home. "At the saloon."

"Didn't y'all close thirty minutes ago?"

"We did. But someone messed with my bike and I

can't get it started."

Even before she got the last word out of her mouth, Luke said, "We'll be there in ten minutes. Five, if I can get Mark to let go of his steak." He hung up before she could tell him to let Mark finish his meal and not to come, that she'd wait for Audrey and Jackson.

With all intentions of calling back and telling them not to bother, Libby hit the redial button. Nothing happened. No bars, no reception. If she wanted to call Luke, she'd have to do it from the landline. She rounded the bar and lifted the phone from the wall mount and quickly dialed the number on the card.

Again, no response. Apparently, Luke was having reception issues on the other end. Great. By the time the boys got there, Audrey and Jackson would probably be sexually satiated and ready to leave.

Then again…maybe not.

The noises in the storeroom increased with loud laughter and even louder groans. The giggles erupted from the doorway and footsteps sounded across the wood flooring, headed for the costume room behind the stage.

Her pussy tightened as Libby imagined the hot sex the two were having and wondered what they were up to now. Envy burned low in her belly. She gathered her purse and strode for the back entrance, forced to pass by the wardrobe room backstage where Audrey kept the costumes for stripper nights. She and Jackson were laughing. The sound of a whip popping captured Libby's attention.

With ten minutes to cool her heels, Libby slowed and paused at the entrance to backstage. A flash of naked skin snagged her attention and she tipped her head to the side to get a better view of what was going on.

Libby's heart fluttered at the sight of Audrey perched on a stack of boxes, completely naked except for her bright red cowboy boots. Her legs wrapped around Jackson's equally naked body as his hips rocked, grinding against hers.

One of Audrey's arms circled Jackson's shoulders as she rode him, leaning close to kiss the side of his neck. In her other hand, she held a long leather whip. She glanced across the room, her gaze connecting with Libby's. Audrey winked and flicked the whip, a loud crack splitting the air.

"Careful with that. You almost got me," Jackson warned.

"Had I been aiming for you, I wouldn't have missed. Now, ride me, cowboy," Audrey demanded.

Libby's breath hitched and she stepped back, just enough so she couldn't see. Heat rose from her chest into her cheeks. She'd never spied on another couple having sex. But Jackson and Audrey had looked so very hot and sexy, and the kink factor of the whip made Libby's blood burn.

Audrey's moan drew Libby back to the entrance like a sailor to a siren. She couldn't help watching as the couple engaged in hot and kinky sex.

Jackson shifted, turning himself and Audrey, giving Libby a side view of the action. His long shaft pumped in and out of Audrey's cunt. The soft slurping sound of a well-lubricated channel interspersed with Audrey's moans and Jackson's grunts as he thrust into her.

Libby's belly tightened. She pressed her hands to still the butterflies, her thighs quivering in anticipation of Jackson's next thrust.

Audrey leaned up to whisper something into Jackson's ear. He smiled down at her and then turned to Libby, his eyelids drooping down over his brown-black eyes. "Wanna join us?"

Libby jumped back, unable to pull her gaze from the couple. "I'm sorry. I didn't mean to watch."

"It's okay. We don't mind." Audrey's ankles crossed behind Jackson's back and she pulled him into her. "Do we?"

Jackson shook his head. "If my lady likes a little more kink, I'm all for it." He waved a hand, beckoning Libby into the room. "She has completely corrupted me."

"No. I shouldn't." Despite her denial, Libby couldn't move back another step—her feet were glued to the floor. The intimate connection between Audrey and Jackson set Libby's pussy on fire. "The twins are coming to pick me up."

Audrey smiled. "You can watch until they come." She let her legs slide down Jackson's thighs to the floor.

Jackson pulled his cock free of Audrey's cunt and it jutted straight out, hard and thick. Bigger than anything Libby had ever witnessed.

She swallowed hard, her tongue slipping across suddenly dry lips.

Audrey trailed a finger all the way down Jackson's chest to the hard, stiff shaft. "Just so you know, the twins are built just like Jackson."

The Kiowa frowned and thrust his hips forward. "I'm bigger."

Audrey slipped off her perch on the boxes and stood before the towering Native American cowboy, running her hand along his cock. "Yes, dear, by far. How's about giving me some of that big dick?"

Jackson's nostrils flared, but he made no move toward Audrey. "Only if you wear these." He reached behind her and snatched a pair of chaps from a hook on the wall. With a quick flick of his wrists, he tied them around her hips.

She glanced toward Libby and whispered, "He has a thing for my red boots and chaps." Her attention focused on her man and her head tipped back, her chin jutting forward. "What if I don't want to wear these old things?"

Despite her words to the contrary, Audrey ran her hands over her lovely, perky breasts and down her narrow waist to where the chaps rested on her hips, as if just wearing the costume made her hot.

"You will do as I say or be punished." Jackson grabbed a leather strap from a shelf and twisted it around Audrey's wrists. Then he spun her to face a metal pole holding up the rack of costumes and lashed her wrists to the bar.

Libby stepped into the room, ready to defend her

boss from the man restraining her. She opened her mouth to protest, but swallowed the words when Audrey smiled over her shoulder.

Her boss called out, "Oh, please, sir, don't tie me up. I promise to do whatever you say."

"Too late." Jackson gave Audrey a stern glare, ruined by the smile quirking at the corners of his lips. "You're mine now, to do with as I wish."

Audrey laughed and tugged against the restraint. "Please, sir."

Then to Libby's shock, Jackson spanked Audrey's naked bottom.

Audrey moaned, her eyes squeezing shut.

Libby took another step into the room, ready to jump on Jackson's back and fight for her boss.

"Do it again," Audrey begged.

Confused, Libby stood stock-still, her mouth hanging open. "I don't understand. Isn't he hurting you?"

"In the very best possible way." Audrey's eyes opened. "Oh, Libby, honey, have you never played games with your lover?"

Libby shook her head. In her former life, she'd never even heard of playing games like this.

"And you call yourself a biker babe?" Audrey shook her head and smiled over her shoulder at Jackson. "Please, sir, I've been very bad. Perhaps you should use the riding crop."

Jackson slipped a riding crop from another hook on the wall and smacked it against his palm.

Libby blinked. "You're not going to use that on her, are you?"

Jackson grinned. "She deserves to be punished." He popped Audrey's ass, leaving a thin red line, not enough to break skin or leave a bruise, but enough Audrey flinched.

Libby flinched with her, imagining the lash of pain. Strangely, her pussy creamed. She covered her mouth to stifle a gasp, her entire body flaming with desire.

"Oh, baby, do it again." Audrey's back curved and her bottom thrust toward Jackson's hand and the waiting crop.

The big cowboy popped her again.

"Oh, yeah," Audrey breathed. "Now, fuck me in the ass, cowboy."

Jackson flung the riding crop on a shelf and grasped Audrey's hips from behind. He slid a finger from her pussy up to her ass, moistening her tightly puckered anus. "Say the magic word."

Audrey moaned. "Please, sir, now." She leaned forward, taking his big cock into her.

So hot she could hardly breathe, Libby took a step backward, then another and finally turned and ran out of the building.

Standing on the back porch to the building, she dragged in deep breaths of warm Texas air. Libby pressed her palm to her aching chest, wishing she had a man she could go to for relief from the raging desire gripping her.

A large hand gripped her elbow and Libby screamed.

"LIBBY, ARE YOU ALL RIGHT?" Mark leaned close to the beautiful redhead, staring into her glazed eyes, concerned at her ragged breathing and flushed cheeks.

Libby glanced up. "Luke?"

He shook his head. "No, I'm Mark."

"I'm here, Libby." Luke strode toward her, his brows narrowing over his forehead. "Are you sure you're okay? You look flushed." He pressed a hand to her forehead. "Are you running a fever?"

Libby gave a bark of choked laughter that didn't quite sound natural. "I'm okay. It's just warm." She fanned her face, tugging at the low neckline of the ribbed-knit tank top, apparently unaware that she was exposing more of her breasts with each tug.

Mark frowned. Something was obviously troubling the woman. "Maybe you should go inside and have a cool drink." He reached for the door handle. "Audrey and Jackson might know what would help."

"No!" Libby snatched at Mark's hand.

His brows rose. "Okay, we won't go inside. But something's wrong and we're worried about you. Is it your bike?"

She glanced toward her damaged bike and blinked, then pressed his hand to her chest, dragging in a deep breath and letting it out before saying, "No, it's not that. I'm fine, really."

The warmth of her breasts against the back of his hand sent a shot of electricity racing through Mark's veins. He had to suck in a deep, steadying stream of air to keep from pulling her into his arms and kissing her.

When she realized where she'd shoved his hand, Libby pushed it to her side, still holding his fingers in a tight grip while she planted a strained smile on her face. "Sorry. I'm just wound up from the night. Could we go?"

Luke pulled her other hand through the crook of his arm and led the threesome toward the pickup truck with the Gray Wolf Design logo printed on the side in bold, artistic lettering. "Maybe you're having an anxiety attack or something. I could take you to a doctor."

"A doctor isn't going to help," Libby muttered. "Only having sex, long and hard, would cure what ails me."

Mark ground to a halt. Had he heard right? "What was that?"

"Nothing, really," she said, a little too fast. "I'm just hot from a long night in the saloon. That's all." The red in Libby's cheeks deepened. Even in the dim lighting from the back porch, Mark could tell her agitation wasn't about the bike.

Libby had definitely mentioned the S.E.X. word and was quick to cover it up. Mark's groin tightened. What had gotten her so hot and bothered? "At least let us stay with you until you cool off, just in case it's more than that." Mark opened the passenger door and held it for Libby.

She stumbled on the running board.

To keep her from falling back, Mark planted a firm hand on her derriere, and half-lifted her into the seat. No sir, touching her ass wasn't helping the erection growing beneath his fly.

Libby slid across the bench seat, and sat in the middle with her hands pressed between her thighs, her face no less red than a few minutes earlier.

"I don't know." Luke sat behind the steering wheel, studying Libby in the light from the dash. "I think we should go back inside and see if Audrey can help. You really are flushed, your cheeks are all red. What do you think, Mark?"

Mark leaned forward in his seat and stared at Libby. Luke was right. The woman had to be running a fever, but it was more than that, and he intended to find out what *it* was. "Yeah. It'll only take a minute for us to run back in. Audrey will know what to do."

Mark and Luke simultaneously reached for their door handles.

"No!" Libby grabbed their shirt sleeves and stopped them before they could descend. "Audrey and Jackson are...are...oh, hell...doing naughty stuff, damn it. Leave them alone."

A slow smile spread across Mark's lips and his boner hardened to steel. "All the more reason to go inside." He clasped his hand around hers. "Come on. Let's go see what's up."

"No, no." Libby pulled her hand free of Mark's.

"I'm good. They're having enough fun without us. No need to butt in."

"But *we* could have so much more fun *with* them." Mark tipped his head. "What's wrong? Afraid you might like it?"

Her eyes widened, her lashes fluttering over the pretty green irises, glowing in the lights from the dash. "Yes, I mean no." She straightened her shoulders and dragged her gaze from Mark's. Refusing to look at either of them, Libby stared straight forward. "Please, let's go."

Mark grinned, his gaze capturing Luke's. "Let's go. Perhaps we can explore that option another time."

Luke shifted into drive and pulled away from the Ugly Stick Saloon.

As they left the parking lot, Libby's body sagged against the seat and she leaned her head back, exposing silky skin stretching all the way down her neck to the swell of her breasts. "Thank God," she breathed.

"For what?" Mark fought to keep from leaning over and kissing the pulse beating wildly at the base of her throat. "My older brother has been known to share."

"I know. They asked me if I wanted to join them." Libby's head came up and she shook it, her long auburn curls brushing across the tops of her shoulders. "I'll never look at chaps the same way, ever again."

Luke laughed out loud. "Did Audrey wear her chaps and red boots?"

"Yes." Libby frowned at him.

"Damn." He smacked his palm against the steering wheel. "We should have stayed."

"It's not too late to go back," Mark insisted, wanting to see Audrey in her chaps almost as much as he wanted to rip Libby's clothes from her body.

"Not tonight." Luke smiled at Libby. "Libby doesn't seem too excited by the possibility of a fivesome."

"Surely after a few minutes, she'd come around," Mark persisted, eager to partake of a little raunchy sex.

"No, it's too soon." Luke shot a frown at Mark. "We have to take it slow with Libby, let *her* call the shots."

"Think she'd be up for a little stargazing?" Mark asked, glancing down at Libby's face. Their talking over her head had to be getting to her by now. He'd kept it up to get a rise out of the woman who'd sat silent for the majority of the conversation. "That meteor shower is tonight."

Libby crossed her arms over her chest. "In case you didn't notice, I'm in the truck with you two. I can hear everything you're saying."

Mark chuckled. She was beautiful when her green eyes flashed daggers. "Then what do you say? Up for a little stargazing?"

Her hands dropped into her lap. "I don't know."

"If we take you home, I doubt you'll go right to sleep, as worked up as you are." Mark grinned. "What with all the excitement going on back at the Ugly Stick."

"Without us," muttered Luke.

Libby's brows dipped and she chewed on her bottom lip. "You promise you won't try anything?"

Mark held up his hands as if in surrender. "Not anything you don't want us to. You can be the master. I even have some handcuffs behind the seat if you want to keep us from touching you."

Luke snorted. "You better take him up on those. Mark isn't known for his ability to keep his hands to himself where a beautiful woman is concerned."

Libby laughed and shook her head. "You two are hard to resist." She sucked in a breath and let it out. "Okay. Stargazing it is, and I'll want those handcuffs… just in case."

"Great." Mark clapped his hands together. "You know the closest spot, right, bro?"

"I do." Luke pressed his foot to the accelerator and sped down the farm-to-market road.

Silence lengthened between the three as the miles passed. Mark's imagination took off, picturing Libby lying in the back of the truck between him and Luke as they stared up at the star-studded, Texas sky.

He'd lean up on his side and brush a hand across her skin, maybe skim the side of her breast.

No sooner had he skimmed her breast in his mind, than he was taking a trip across her belly and into her panties. "Oh, yeah. We're going to see a lot tonight."

"Of stars, Mark. Stars." Libby pressed a hand to his thigh.

That wouldn't be all they'd see if Mark had his wicked way with her.

# CHAPTER THREE

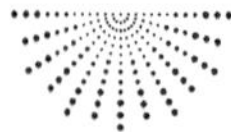

*L*ibby sat between the two men, her heart beating like a snare drum in a rock band, as Luke turned off the pavement onto a gravel road, winding upward to the top of a hill.

When the vehicle came to a halt, Libby's breathing grew shallower and her fingers gripped the hem of her tank top, twisting the fabric. A lot could happen with nothing but the three of them and the open night sky. The endless possibilities rose up in Libby's chest and thumped hard against her rib cage.

"Two years," she whispered.

Luke turned off the engine. "What was two years?"

"Nothing." Libby bit down on her tongue. Hell, she'd said it out loud. How pathetic. Biker babes didn't go two years without sex. Some tough gal she was.

"There!" Mark pointed to the sky. "Did you see it?"

A flash skimmed across the sky. Libby leaned

forward to peer out the windshield as the light extinguished. "I did. I saw it." She smiled at Mark, the swell of joy rising inside, alongside the residual sexual tension still lingering from her voyeuristic foray into Audrey and Jackson's love life. "I believe that's the first shooting star I've ever seen."

"You don't get out much, do you?" Mark commented. "We see them all the time around here."

"Can't see the stars where I'm from," she said, regretting her slip as soon as it was made.

"And where is it you can't see the stars?" Luke glanced at her, his brows dipping. "Which city?"

Mark scratched his chin. "I believe she mentioned New York City earlier this evening."

"The city doesn't matter." Libby smiled at him. "Are we going to see some stars, or what?"

Mark's grin widened. "Now you're talking." He dropped to the ground and held out his hands to Libby. He grabbed her around the waist and swung her to the ground, kissing her on the lips, in a brief, easy display of affection.

Libby envied his relaxed view on sex.

For all the black leather and motorcycle, Libby was still her father's daughter, trapped in a prudish world of proper behavior for a debutante. She had to remind herself that those days were over. She could be whomever she wanted to be, now that she was Libby Jones.

Luke tipped the truck seat forward and pulled a blanket out. "Let's get set up. Sorry we don't have any refreshments."

"I don't need any." Libby tipped her head back, staring up at the heavens. "I've been sipping on ginger ale and munching on pretzels all night. I just want fresh air and shooting stars."

"Can't guarantee the meteor shower, but there's plenty of fresh air to go around." Luke shook out the blanket and waved a hand for her to take a seat. "Your magic carpet awaits."

With a million stars twinkling down on them in a clear, black Texas sky, Libby could almost believe the blanket might hold a little enchantment for her. Add two handsome Kiowa cowboys to the scenario, and her excitement mounted. She sat in the middle of the blanket, her knees drawn up to her chin, hands clasped around her calves to keep her fingers from shaking. A difficult task when her entire body trembled.

Mark dropped down beside her, running a hand down her bare arm. "Cold?"

"Not at all." Libby shivered, despite her denial.

"You're trembling." Luke sat down beside her. "You're not scared of us, are you?"

Libby sat up straighter, propping her arms behind her and stretching her legs out in an effort to look nonchalant. "Of course not." Afraid of herself? You bet.

Luke lay back on the blanket. "You know we're not out here to take advantage of you."

"You're not?" Libby couldn't help the way her shoulders sagged at Luke's announcement. Now that she was here, she'd hoped they'd take complete advantage of her and end her long dry spell.

"Unless you want us to," Mark added, his fingers skimming along the outside of Libby's thigh.

Oh she wanted all right. She forced a shrug to keep from appearing too eager. "I'll keep that thought in mind." Then she lay back next to Luke, linking her fingers over her middle. "I don't think I've ever seen as many stars."

"It's one of the things we love so much about this little piece of heaven we call Texas." Mark rested on his side, facing Libby, staring at her, not the sky.

Luke turned her way and leaned up on an elbow. "We don't get a lot of light pollution. The only times Temptation and Hole in the Wall get all lit up is during the Friday night football games in the fall. The rest of the year, it's like this."

"Do you two go to the football games?" she asked.

"As often as we can." Mark smiled. "We'll take you next time they have one."

Libby's heart squeezed tightly. Although it was late summer, the football season wouldn't start for another month. By then, she'd be on the road again.

Libby studied the men on either side of her, recalling the image of Jackson's huge penis and Audrey's assurance the Gray Wolf brothers were built alike.

Her tongue snaked out to moisten her lips, heat surging throughout her body.

Why not have a little fun during her last few days in Temptation? What would it hurt? Before long, she'd be gone, the twins would move on and at least she'd have scratched that itch and broken her dry spell. Her stomach turned cartwheels, her hands growing warm and clammy.

Still excited from witnessing the antics of Jackson and Audrey and even more determined to make the most of this night, she dragged in a deep breath and let it out slowly. That residual sexual desire flared to an inferno, reminding Libby that she was young, single and horny as hell. She toed off her boots and ran her bare foot up Mark's leg, ready to get the party started. Then she dropped her voice to a low sexy drawl. "Speaking of games…what do you two do for fun, when you're not dancing at the Ugly Stick, watching football and working? Where do you take your women when the saloon is closed?"

LUKE'S GROIN TIGHTENED. He couldn't believe Libby was actually showing interest by gracing Mark with the foot action. For the longest time Libby had put up roadblocks and detour signs when it came to any advances they'd tried to make. She'd pretty much spelled it out that she wasn't interested in a relationship with the Gray Wolf brothers, or anyone else, for that matter.

From the first time he and Mark had spotted her at the Ugly Stick Saloon, they'd argued over who would go after her. Finally he and Mark agreed that if Libby was willing to be shared between them, great. A ménage could be much more erotic and sexually satisfying for all parties involved. Still, it might be too soon to spring that one on her.

Luke cleared his throat. "Despite public perception, we don't do much other than a dinner date now and then."

"Hey, man, don't make her think we're losers or something." Mark ran a hand along Libby's leather-clad thigh. "We just don't take them home. We find other interesting places to go."

"Like out to watch the stars?" Libby's foot stilled on its rise up Mark's leg.

Luke traced a finger along her cheek. "Not until now. This is a first. Usually we go down by the lake and do a little skinny-dipping."

Libby relaxed, her foot continuing its path along Mark's calf, one of her hands brushing against Luke's crisp white shirt, dipping into the gap between buttons. "Ever share a woman between you?" She slid her tongue slowly along her full bottom lip.

Luke choked back a whoop, his pulse leaping at the obvious invitation. "We have, but they were never real relationships, just sex." He shrugged. "We're twins. We tend to work out our differences, come up with compromises. Because we were both attracted to you, we didn't want to fight about it. We agreed to let you decide on one or the other or… both of us."

Mark laughed. "My brother, the diplomat. He's always been the calm one."

Libby's brows rose. "Is that so?" She shifted, removing her foot from Mark's leg and placing the other foot on Luke's. "What does it take to shatter his calm?"

"That about does it." Luke's Adam's apple bobbed as he swallowed hard. His cock jerked behind the zipper of his jeans, hardening in seconds, straining against the denim.

"Show me what's it like to have two men who look so much alike make love to one woman."

Luke frowned, waiting for the catch. After all this time, Libby was willing to have sex with both of them, not just flirt? "Are you sure?"

Mark reached across Libby and punched his brother in the shoulder. "You're looking a gift horse in the mouth." Mark's fist loosened and he dropped his hand to Libby's abdomen. "Not that you're a horse, by any means. But if the lady wants both, give her both. Sheesh." His fingers spread out across her belly and inched upward to cup a full, rounded breast in his palm.

Not to be outdone, Luke rested a hand on her belly where his brother's had been a moment before. "We don't want to scare you off on our first date."

Libby frowned.

Uh-oh. Luke's gut tightened…here came the catch.

"Let me get a few things straight…" She reached down and tugged the hem of her shirt, lifting it up and over her head. "This is not a date. We are not in a relationship, and I'm not staying."

Luke's hand met warm, silky skin. "Not staying? You might want to put your top back on before you head back to town."

She laughed, the sound tight. "I'm staying here, for now. But I'm not staying for long in Temptation."

"Why?" Mark asked, his fingers finding the tip of her nipple through her bra. "Don't you like us?"

Her hand cupped the back of his. "Too much. And if either one of you asks another question, the night will be over."

Luke didn't like it. A thousand questions stirred in his mind and he opened his mouth several times, but bit down hard on his tongue, rather than spoil the evening. "Okay, no questions. I suppose we'll just have to guess what you like."

"Um. Now you're getting the idea." She lay back, a smile slipping across her face.

Mark slid the strap of her bra down her shoulder, peeling the cup back from one breast. "Can't ask a question. Hmm. Maybe the lady will like this?" He bent low, licked her nipple then blew a stream of air across the tip.

The smooth round areola puckered into a tight nubbin.

Libby gasped. "Yes, the lady likes that."

Luke's hand slipped downward to the waistband of her leather pants, flipping the button loose and sliding the zipper downward. He leaned over her belly, kissing a path toward the open fly and the black lace panties. "I like this."

"Me, too." Libby reached down, twining her fingers in Luke's hair, angling his head lower. "I like it even better without the clothes."

"As you wish." Luke gripped the hem of her leather

pants and tugged them down her legs, over her calves and off the end of her feet. Which left the panties. These he removed a little slower, relishing the reveal of the triangle of brownish-red curls covering her pussy. "This, I like a lot." He pressed a kiss to the puff of curls.

Libby's knees parted, falling to either side, exposing her damp cunt to Luke, the moisture of her juices glistening in the starlight.

Luke's cock pressed hard against the constriction of his jeans. He paused to adjust himself, glancing up Libby's body to where his brother was taking his time with Libby's breasts.

Mark bent to take her nipple in his mouth, sucking on it gently.

Luke's mouth watered, anxious to taste Libby's delights in an entirely different place.

Libby pushed up to her elbows, a pretty frown wrinkling her brows. "You two have the advantage."

Mark laughed. "I thought that was the idea."

"Not exactly." Her brows rose and she stared from Luke back to Mark. "You're still wearing all your clothes." She reached behind her and flicked the clasp on her bra and shimmied out of it, the last barrier between her and the night air. "And I'm completely naked."

Luke beat Mark to his feet, flicking the buttons on his shirt so fast, a couple popped off.

Mark stripped his jeans first, forgetting to remove his boots until too late. He stumbled, falling to the ground.

Libby laughed, the sound filling the night with a joy that warmed Luke's heart.

As he stripped the shirt from his back and the boots from his feet, he knew he couldn't let this be their last time together. Libby was an amazing woman—strong, yet vulnerable, beautiful and sensitive. She deserved to laugh all the time. As he shucked his jeans and lay down beside her, he smoothed a hand along her face, staring down into her eyes.

Mark was still wrestling with his boots and working at the buttons on his shirt.

Luke kissed her temple. "You should laugh more often."

The smile died on her lips. "I haven't had much to laugh about for a long time."

"What—"

She pressed a finger to his lips. "Don't ask…remember?"

He nodded, the need to know everything about this woman so strong, Luke thought he'd bust a gut holding back. "Fair enough." Instead, he released all his pent-up emotion into a single kiss, claiming her mouth, his tongue pushing past her teeth to stroke the length of hers. She tasted of pretzels and ginger ale. Sweet and salty, and more intoxicating than any alcoholic drink Luke had ever consumed. "I could kiss you forever and never get enough."

She wrapped her fingers around the back of his neck and pulled him down for another. Before their lips met, she said, "Forget forever. Kiss me like there's no tomorrow."

Luke complied, his fingers threading through her hair, his mouth crushing hers in an attempt to get even closer.

Libby's arms circled his neck, a soft, naked leg swept alongside his, curling around his hip.

"Eh-hem. Let me kiss her next." Mark's hand on Luke's shoulder reminded him that this was a chance for both of them to show Libby what making love to twins could be like.

Luke pressed another quick kiss to Libby's lips and leaned back.

"That was amazing." Libby's arms unwound from Luke's neck.

"You haven't seen anything yet." Luke winked at Mark as his brother hovered behind Libby. "Mark's known for his magical lips."

Libby raised her arm behind her to cup the back of Mark's neck and turned her head toward him. "I'll be the judge."

While Mark made his mark on her lips, Luke smoothed his hand over Libby's arm and down to capture a breast in his palm, weighing the full swell. He bent to take the nipple, sucking it deeply into his mouth, flicking at the tip with his tongue. God, she was beautiful, sexy and beguiling. He nudged the side of her hip with his cock, eager to plunge into her warm wetness. But he knew he had to take it slowly, show Libby he and his brother weren't animals. No matter how hard it would be to hold back and not slake the hunger building like molten lava in a volcano.

Luke abandoned the breast and kissed a path over her ribs, down to her flat belly, his fingers threaded through the hairs at the apex of her thighs, probing for the treasure beneath. When he parted her folds and flicked her clitoris, he unleashed the wanton woman.

Her back arched and she cried out, the sound muffled my Mark's mouth.

Dipping lower, Luke plunged his finger into her cunt, swirled it around in the juices and trailed it back up to the swollen bud of nerves. Libby writhed against the blanket with every touch.

Mark moved around to Libby's front, taking care of her breasts while Luke maneuvered between the woman's legs, lifting her bottom so that he could plunge his tongue into her pussy, lapping up the sweet, musky juices. Then he turned his attention to her clit, laving it with slow, steady strokes, over and over, increasing the speed. He slipped one finger into her channel, then another, all the while licking her nubbin of desire, refusing to let up until he had her screaming out loud with pleasure.

Libby could barely breathe. With one brother between her legs and the other massaging her breasts, the sensations were spiraling around her, bombarding her with so much pleasure, she feared she'd die—and what a glorious death it would be.

Luke's relentless assault on the special place that had gone untouched by a man for two years had her lit up like fireworks on the fourth of July. As she rock-eted to the edge, she clutched Luke's hair with one hand and the back of Mark's with the other, her fingers digging into their scalps. As she pitched over the top, she screamed, calling out their names, her body trembling, each spasm more explosive than the last.

Before she could tumble back to earth, Libby rolled over, coming up on her hands and knees. She wrapped her hand around Mark's engorged cock and slid up the length and off the end. "I want you both." She raised her ass as high as she could while tugging on Mark's length, urging him to get closer. "Let me pleasure one, while the other pleasures me."

Luke reached for his jeans, pulling his wallet from the back pocket.

Libby breathed a sigh when Luke pulled a foil packet out, tore it open and slipped the rubber down over his straining member.

"I must say, I'm glad you boys come prepared," she said. No matter how much she wanted these men to make love to her, her head was too foggy to remember her own name, much less have a conversa-tion about sexually transmitted diseases.

"I've got another in my wallet." Mark rose to his knees in front of her, his cock jutting straight out, eager and ready for anything.

Libby smiled. "Good. I think we're going to need it." She ran a hand from the tip of his dick, down the full, thick length to his balls, rolling them between her fingers.

"Damn right, we will." Mark grabbed her hair, his fingers twisting around the strands. "Tell me how rough you want it, sweetheart."

An image of Jackson and the riding crop rose in Libby's mind and made her shudder with need. Shocked at how her pulse leaped at the mention of playing rough, Libby gulped and answered with her best biker-babe confidence. "I can take anything you have to dish out. The rougher, the better."

Mark laughed and shoved her head downward, thrusting his cock into her mouth. "Then take it in the mouth, biker girl."

"Mark…" Luke warned.

Libby nearly laughed, except she was so tied in knots over being treated so coarsely, she retreated off the end of Mark's dick. For the first time in her life, she assumed the role of a sex-starved whore, eager for some cock, which wasn't far off the truth. "Talk dirty all you want, cowboy." She glanced over her shoulder, her brows cocked. "Are you going to point that thing or shoot?" Her pussy practically dripped in anticipation of Luke's cock burying itself inside her.

"You're mouthy, woman." Luke slapped her ass, the sound louder than the sting.

The slight pain made Libby draw in her breath, amazed at how good it actually felt. Her father would be aghast. "You call that punishment?" She forced a shaky laugh before sucking Mark's cock back into her mouth.

Luke slapped harder.

The sting of his fingers on her ass sent a wash of come trickling to the edge of her opening.

"I'll fuck you, baby, like there's no tomorrow." Luke thrust his big, thick cock into her, filling her pussy, stretching her channel so tight, she could barely move.

Libby held her breath, her teeth scraping the length of Mark's member.

"Careful, sweetheart. No biting." Mark yanked her head toward him. "But don't stop now." He pumped in and out of her mouth, while Luke drove deep inside her.

The balmy night air teased her nipples, the stars above added just the right amount of lighting and the sex couldn't have been more perfect. Libby had fantasized many times, but never engaged in sex games while making love. She'd always played by the rules of polite society, living in her concrete castle at the top of a skyscraper in New York City.

She'd done what her father demanded, attending all the right schools, having all the right friends and agreeing to marry the man her father approved of, a junior partner at her father's firm.

Never had she stepped out of line. Never would she have dreamed of deviant behavior such as what she was experiencing now. And all she could think of was why she hadn't done this sooner? Who knew she'd like rough sex? That she'd like being fucked like an animal while sucking on another man's cock? Her transformation from socialite to biker chick had been only a shadow of what she could achieve.

Making love to the Gray Wolf twins put her on an entirely different level. And damn it, she wanted more.

While Luke pumped her like a piston, he leaned over her, his fingers seeking out and finding the center of her pleasure, that swollen, throbbing bundle of nerve endings. He stroked her, bringing her along with him as he stiffened, his cock cleaving deeper, faster and more powerfully. He flicked her clit in rhythm, grinding to an abrupt halt, his one hand on her hip, digging in, holding her ass to his groin as his member pulsed inside her.

Mark's hips moved faster and faster, his fingers tightening in Libby's hair. He bumped against the back of her throat, once, twice and he pulled free.

Libby gasped, dragging in air, her arms collapsing beneath her. "Why didn't you come?"

Mark grinned, holding his cock in his hand, stroking its hardened length. "Saving it for later."

Libby pressed her face against the blanket, her ass high in the air, still connected in the most intimate way to Luke. "That was amazing."

Luke disengaged, assisting her to lie on the blanket, spooning her backside.

Mark lay in front of her, gathering her hands in his. "You are the amazing one."

"You think I'm done for the night?" Libby pressed his hands to her dripping core. "Feel that?"

"God, yes." His fingers slid into her. "So wet."

"I could easily go another round, as long as you have protection."

Mark let out a loud whoop and rolled away from her, making a grab for his wallet.

"You can wait until next time, if you're sore." Luke hugged her from behind, his hand rising to cup a breast. He nuzzled her ear, his warm breath and gentle words stirring her heart more than gratifyingly raunchy sex.

She pressed his hand closer, guiding him to pinch her nipple. "No. I'm not too sore."

Mark turned, condom in hand, his eyes wide and eager. "I can wait." He sighed. "Really." His cock twitched, still stiff and straight.

"Remember what I said? Love me like there's no tomorrow." Libby held out her hand for the contraceptive. "Don't waste a minute of the time we have together." She tore the foil with her teeth then slipped the rubber over Mark's cock. "Now, let's fuck," she said, the coarse word rolling off her tongue like a new and tasty treat.

Mark lay down beside her, pressing his cock between her thighs.

Libby draped her leg over his, giving him access, her hand on his hip, guiding him home.

He rammed into her in one long, solid slide.

Libby held her breath until he'd gone as far as he could. Then she let out a shaky sigh. "You Gray Wolfs are almost too much."

Mark jerked back. "Let me know if it hurts."

Her fingers dug into his buttocks. "No, it's good. Big, sexy…incredibly good."

Luke nuzzled the curve of her throat, his hand on her breast teasing and massaging.

Mark settled into smooth, easy strokes, taking it slow and gentle.

"What happened to the rough riders?" Libby asked. "I thought you two liked playing rough."

"We do, for the most part." Mark brushed his lips over hers. "But sometimes it's better to take our time. It makes it even better when we're making love like there's no tomorrow."

Libby's heart contracted and tears welled in her eyes before she could control them. She squeezed them shut. "Make it count, boys. Make it count."

Mark crushed her mouth with his, slanting over her as he increased the pressure and speed of his thrusts.

Luke's damp cock slid between her butt cheeks, making use of the crease as he mimicked his brother's motions. His hands roved over her ribs and down to the furry mound, finding and tickling the bud buried between her folds.

Libby moaned, her hand covering Luke's, pressing it against her clit. "You're making it so hard."

His lips caressed the skin on the back of her neck. "You're making *us* hard."

Her mouth curved into a sad smile. "Hard for me to forget that there is no tomorrow."

Mark's hands gripped her hips as he thrust into her one last time, holding her still as his body shook with his release. "There has to be a tomorrow. Tonight was unforgettable."

A single tear slipped from the corner of her eye, falling to the blanket, unnoticed. Libby had to go. She thought that all the towns she'd been through would have toughened her to the next move, but this one would be the hardest.

If she stayed, she risked falling, deeply and hopelessly in love. She feared she might already have committed that folly. Tomorrow she'd break the news to Audrey. The Ugly Stick Saloon would be short one bartender.

# CHAPTER FOUR

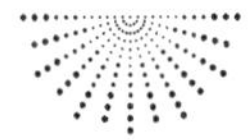

"She's special." Luke glanced at the embarrassingly large bouquet of flowers balanced between Mark's legs in the front seat of the pickup. "Are you sure daisies are special enough?"

"For the tenth time, they're perfect." Mark wanted to laugh out loud at his normally calm, cool and collected brother. "You're as nervous as a cat in a room full of rocking chairs. What's the worst that could happen?"

"She could tell us to take a hike."

"Then it wasn't meant to be."

Luke's palm smacked against the steering wheel. "Damn it, Mark, be serious for once."

Mark did laugh this time. But he sobered quickly at the frown on his brother's forehead. "She told us last night that there might not be any tomorrows for us. I'm trying not to set myself up for disappointment." His words were empty. If Libby refused to see them again, he'd be eaten up with all kinds of disappointment. The woman had more than captured his lusty attention, her inner vulnerability threatened his carefree lifestyle, making him think of a happily ever after for the first time in his life.

Dusk had settled into darkness, made more profound by a clouded sky. Not one for superstition, Mark tried to ignore the portent of something unpleasant to come, telling himself the clouds were pure coincidence. "Look, we give her the flowers, remind her of our offer to go riding tomorrow and then we back off. If she wants to see us again, she'll show."

"If not?" Luke's foot slipped off the accelerator and the truck slowed. "If she doesn't want to see us…if we came on too strong…if we scared her way?"

"As Jackson would say, *don't borrow trouble*." Mark stared down at the flowers, praying the daisies were the right flower, that Libby would be happy to get them and she'd come with them the next day on their ride.

Luke glanced across at Mark. "I want to show her our place."

Mark nodded. "Me, too. I don't want to run her off with too much too soon."

Luke drew in a deep breath and let it out, his shoulders straightening. "We'll have to take it a step at a time. Obviously, something's spooked her. For all her bad-ass ways, Libby is a marshmallow—a sweet, incredibly beautiful marshmallow—and we have to make sure we don't crush her."

Mark nodded. "Right. Maybe we should talk to Audrey first."

"Good idea." Luke pulled into the parking lot of the Ugly Stick Saloon and swung around to the rear of the building, parking beside Libby's motorcycle.

"Looks like she got it fixed."

"Makes me feel a whole lot better knowing she's not stranded." Luke's fingers tightened on the steering wheel. "I'd sure like to get my hands around the throat of the guy who vandalized it."

"You and me both."

"Come on, let's find the boss." Luke led the way through the back door, passing the costume room and stopping at the storeroom.

A smile quirked Mark's lips at the thought of his older brother banging the saloon owner in that room. As soon as his mind conjured an image of Jackson and Audrey naked and doing it, he imagined himself, Libby and Luke naked amongst the stacks of liquor boxes, doing all kinds of naughty things. "I'm getting a hard-on just thinking about her," Mark said out loud, adjusting his jeans to accommodate the rising ridge behind his fly.

"Keep it in your pants, brother." Luke adjusted himself.

"I notice you're not so unaffected." Mark patted Luke's back. "Yeah, I can't get her off my mind either."

"What are you two boys doing back here?" Greta Sue, the best bar bouncer since Jack "Hammerfist" McKenzie, stepped into the hallway from the front of the saloon, crossing her arms over her linebacker chest.

"Hey, Greta Sue." Mark gave her one of his most charming grins. "You're looking beautiful tonight."

"Cut the crap, Gray Wolf." Although her words were tough, Greta Sue's hand rose to pat the dull blond hair she had pulled back in a prison-warden bun. She had a soft place in her tough-gal chest for the Gray Wolf brothers, ever since Jackson Gray Wolf had become her boss's sweetheart.

"We need to see Audrey," Luke said. "It's an emergency."

Greta Sue tipped her head to the side, peering around behind the men. "I don't see a fire or police."

"It's worse." Mark pulled the bouquet of flowers from behind his back. "It's matters of the heart."

Greta Sue's forehead creased into a frown. "Does Jackson know about this?" She crossed ham-hock sized arms over her chest. "'Cause I'm not likin' this one bit. Jackson and Audrey are made for each other. I haven't see that woman happier since she bought this junkyard."

Mark laughed and clapped a hand to Greta Sue's back. When she glared at him through slitted eyes, he immediately withdrew his arm as if she might bite it off. "No, we're not interested in stealing Audrey away from Jackson. We need her advice about someone else."

Greta Sue remained stiff for a full two seconds longer before she relaxed, her arms falling to her side. "In that case, you can find her out front."

"Uh…could you get her for us?" Luke asked. "We'd kinda like to speak to her in private, not in front of that bar full of rednecks."

Greta Sue frowned. "What do I look like, a gopher?"

"No, ma'am." Mark plucked a daisy out of the bouquet. "You look like a wonderful woman who still believes in the power of love." He handed her the daisy. "Please, Greta Sue."

The hardened bouncer took the daisy. She could easily have snapped the fragile stem in her fingers; instead, she stared down at the flower. "Don't ever let it be said that I'm one to stand in the way of love." She glanced up at Mark. "And you owe me, big time."

"He'll do whatever you want, just get Audrey," Luke implored.

"I'll be collecting." Greta Sue's gaze traveled Mark's length, then she spun and headed into the bar.

Mark backhanded his brother in the gut. "Thanks for promising the world to Greta Sue, at my expense."

"We have to talk to Audrey."

"Still…"

Audrey rounded the corner from the direction of the bar, eyes blazing, her fists clenched.

"Audrey, we—" Luke started.

"Not a word." She pointed to the storeroom. "In there. Now."

Mark snapped to attention and entered the room as directed, Luke following so close he bumped into Mark's back.

As soon as Audrey closed the door, she spun to

face them, a full head shorter, but still intimidating with her fists perched on her hips. "What in the hell did you do to my best bartender last night?"

Mark stepped forward. "What do you mean?"

"When she came in today, she handed me her resignation. Out of the friggin' blue, damn it. And the goddamn rodeo is in town this weekend."

"Holy hell." Luke spun and paced the short length of the room, running a hand through his hair. "She wasn't kidding."

"Kidding? Kidding about what?" The bright pink splotches on Audrey's cheeks deepened into red. "You two owe me an explanation. I couldn't get anything out of Libby except a muttered, lame excuse and a bucket of tears."

Mark set the bouquet of flowers on a box and took Audrey's hand. "We made love to her."

Luke spun and strode back to where Mark and Audrey stood. "Purely consensual. And she was amazing."

Audrey snorted. "Apparently, she didn't feel the same."

Beside his ego taking a full sucker punch to his lower gut, Mark couldn't fathom what had gone wrong.

"Was there foreplay? Did you make sure she liked what you were doing? Did you bother to ask her what she liked? Did you get to know her before you nailed the girl?" Audrey drilled.

"We did everything right, as far as I could tell," Luke said. "She didn't complain."

Mark shook his head. "Not everything. She wouldn't let us get to know her better."

Audrey pounced on Mark, her finger poking into his chest. "What do you mean?"

Mark grabbed Audrey's finger and held it away from him. "When we tried to ask her about herself, she shut us down."

"Damn." Audrey's lips twisted. She shook her head, finger-combing her long blond hair back from her forehead. "I should have seen this coming."

"Seen what?" Luke grabbed Audrey's arms, spinning her to face him. "What do you know about Libby? What's she hiding?"

Audrey brushed Luke's hands from her arms. "I don't know. She never opened up to me. From all that I've gathered, she's running from something."

Mark's heart sank into his chest. He and Luke had suspected the same. "From what?"

"If I knew, I'd have done something about it." Audrey sighed. "What are we going to do?"

"What about her job application?" Luke asked. "Did she list any previous experience… references…anything?"

"When I hired her eight months ago, I didn't ask for any. She was able to mix all the drinks, had the figure to wear a tank top, and she looked like she'd just lost her favorite dog. I couldn't turn her away. Hell, I would have put her to work busing tables rather than let her leave. She looked like she could use a friend."

"And in eight months you don't know anything else about her? Does she have family?"

Audrey shook her head. "Not that I know of."

Mark asked the question that jumped to the forefront of his mind. "Is she married?"

"She isn't wearing a ring, nor does she show any indication of a past ring. Hell, I thought she was a lesbian for the longest, when she turned down every guy in the joint. Until I saw that she turned down the women as well."

"She's afraid of something." Luke crossed his arms over his chest.

"What can she possibly be afraid of?" Audrey dug her hands into her back pockets. "I don't know anything about her past, just what I've seen since she got here. I don't want to lose her. She's not just my best bartender, she's my friend. I feel responsible for her."

Mark sat on a box, starring at the bouquet of flowers. "Why would she want to leave now?"

Audrey's brows knit. "When she told me she was leaving, she said something about staying too long."

"Eight months?" Luke smacked his cowboy hat against his knee. "We're just getting to know her. How can eight months be too long?"

"I don't know. It's as if she wants to keep moving to keep her past from catching up." Audrey glanced across at Mark. "It *has* to be that she's running from something or someone."

"Libby might not even be her real name."

"I don't care what her real name is. She's real enough to me." Mark stood. "We can't just let her go."

"How long of a notice did she give you?" Luke asked.

"She wanted to quit after tonight." Audrey rocked back on her heels. "I made her promise to wait until after the Cowboy Masquerade Ball."

"That gives us two days to figure this out." Mark's gaze connected with Luke's. "Which also means we don't have much time to convince her to stay."

"Anything you can do." Audrey touched Mark's arm. "She's never going to have a life until she stops running and faces whatever has her scared."

Mark hefted the bouquet of flowers and handed them to Audrey. "Will you give these to her and tell her they are from her secret admirers?"

Audrey smiled. "Daisies. They're so wild and free, yet delicate and pure." She nodded. "Nice touch. Are you two staying?"

"Only long enough to say hello to Libby." Mark opened the door to the storeroom. "We'll do our best to get her to stay."

"What about the flowers? When should I give them to her?"

"Wait until after we leave." Luke strode from the storeroom and entered the bar.

Mark followed on his heels, grateful his stoic twin was back on his game. The thought of losing Libby after just finding her must have shocked him into his usual calm, determined self.

All of the seats at the bar were filled, and Libby's

head was down as she measured whiskey into shot glasses.

Luke headed for the table where their older brother, Jackson, sat alone, nursing a beer.

Mark took the seat on one side of Jackson and Luke dropped into the other.

"What are you two up to tonight?" Jackson waved to Kendall Mason, one of the sexy beauties who waited tables at the Ugly Stick Saloon. "A beer for my brothers."

The music blared to life and the early patrons filled the dance floor, shuffling along to a raucous Texas two-step.

A brunette Mark had danced with the night before stopped in front of him. "Wanna dance?"

Mark smiled up at her, not wanting to hurt her feelings, but not the least bit interested in any other woman besides Libby now that he and Luke had broken past her initial barriers. "Not tonight, but thanks."

She shrugged and turned to Luke. "How about you?"

Luke shook his head, craning his neck to see around her. "Not dancing tonight." He glanced toward a table full of rednecks. "Why not ask RJ? He's the best dancer in this bar."

"If I wanted to dance with RJ, I'd have asked him first." The woman flipped her hair over her shoulder and stalked away.

Jackson's brows rose up into the hair hanging

down over his forehead. "Why aren't you two up dancing?"

Mark tipped his head toward the bar.

About that time, Libby looked up, her gaze connecting with his.

Mark's groin tightened, his stomach flipping over. He pressed a hand to his belly.

"Did you feel that?" Luke asked, pressing his palm to his own gut.

"Felt like a punch to the gut," Mark acknowledged.

"You two are pathetic." Jackson chuckled and took a deep swallow of his beer. "If you like her that much, tell her."

Mark sighed. "It's not that easy."

"She says she's leaving town," Luke added.

Jackson stared from Mark to Luke and back again. "What did you do to the girl?"

"Get Audrey to fill you in on the details. Right now we need to check into a few things."

"Like?" Jackson set his mug on the table.

"We need you to call in a favor from your buddy in the sheriff's department."

Their brother's brows furrowed. "Dusty Cramer?"

"Yeah, Cramer." Luke leaned forward. "We need him to search through the missing persons database and see if he finds Libby Jones, or someone fitting her description."

"Why don't you ask him yourself?" Jackson asked.

Luke poked a finger at Mark. "He's never forgiven Romeo here for stealing his prom date."

"Hell, that was a long time ago, you'd think he'd have forgotten all about that," Mark groused.

"Point is," Luke continued, "he hasn't."

Jackson swallowed another gulp of beer before responding to their request. "I'll see what I can do."

"Could you make it fast? Libby's leaving soon. We need to know why she's running."

"What if you find out something you don't like?" Jackson pulled out his phone and thumbed through his contacts. "What if there's a warrant out for her arrest?"

Mark glanced across at Libby. "Then I'll be leaving with her."

"And me," Luke added.

"Crazy, stupid love." Jackson glanced down at his phone and shook his head. "No reception." He stood and headed for the office at the back of the bar, calling back over his shoulder. "Can't say as I blame you. I'd take a bullet for Audrey."

After their brother walked out, the waitress arrived with a tray, bearing two mugs of beer.

Mark downed half of his before he set the mug on the table.

Luke left his untouched. "What now?"

"We remind her of our date to go riding tomorrow. It's our last chance to woo her."

His fingers drumming against the table, Luke stared across at the woman foremost in their minds. "What about tonight?"

Mark wanted nothing more than to beat off every man crowded around the bar and snatch Libby away from the noise. "She has to be exhausted after staying up last night, and shouting over the music won't help get our message across."

Luke nodded. "We can't even get close to her, not with that pack of yahoos sniffing around her."

"Then we wait for her to go on break." Mark downed the rest of his beer and headed for the door.

Luke followed. "That could take a long time."

Mark cocked a smile at his brother. "She's worth the wait."

"Absolutely." Luke led the way outside to their pickup, dropping the tailgate. "Have a seat."

Mark sat beside his brother. "What do you think?"

"About Libby leaving?" Luke removed his cowboy hat and ran a hand through his hair. "It blows."

"No kidding." Mark leaned back and stared up at the stars. "I've gone over and over everything she said, everything we did."

"Same." Luke leaned back on his hands. "Were we too pushy? Did we overwhelm her? Was she ready for the two of us at once?"

Mark sighed. "At the time it all felt…"

"Right," Luke finished.

"She's running from something."

"God, I hope it's not a husband."

"You and me both." Mark sat forward, slapping his hat against his leg. "Can you picture her at our place?"

Luke straightened, cramming his cowboy hat on his head. "I've done nothing but envision her at Skyview."

Mark pushed off the end of the tailgate and stood. "It's the perfect place for her...for the three of us."

"She's a special woman."

"Are you still okay with sharing a woman between the two of us?" Mark asked.

Luke's lips quirked upward in a smile. "As long as it's Libby."

"That's what I'm thinking." Mark rocked back on his heels, his thumbs hooked into his belt loops, images of Libby lying naked under the stars. "Do you think she'd be willing to be with both of us for the long run?"

Luke's gaze met Mark's. "She was with both of us last night. Like I told Audrey, I didn't hear any complaints."

Mark's lips twisted, a sinking feeling filling his gut. "And look where that went."

"Right." Luke's shoulders sagged. "Turned in her notice."

One of Libby's remarks from the previous night slipped into Mark's thoughts. "Remember, even before we touched her, she'd said she wanted us to make love to her like there's no tomorrow."

"Yes, she did." Luke stared across at his brother. "More than once."

A lonely, sad feeling squeezed Mark's chest until it hurt. He pressed a hand to the soreness. "Reckon she knew she'd be quitting the saloon?"

"I reckon so." Luke shook his head. "Might even be why she decided to have a fling with us."

"We can't let it end." Mark slammed a palm to his thigh. "Not now that we've found her."

"She's got a right to leave," Luke reminded him.

"But we could be so much more than a tumble in the hay."

"Not if she has her way and skips out of town."

"We can't let her go." Mark clenched both hands into fists. "Think she'll come riding with us tomorrow? Might be our only shot at changing her mind."

"I don't know. Why don't we ask her?" Luke nodded toward the back door of the saloon.

Libby exited, closing the door behind her before leaning against it, pushing a hand through her hair. The yellow light over the back door glanced off her coppery curls, forming a kind of halo around her.

Mark's breath lodged in his throat. "God, she's beautiful," he whispered, stepping out.

Luke slid off the tailgate and laid a hand on Mark's shoulder, bringing him to a halt. "Play it cool, man. We don't want her to run."

"I got this."

# CHAPTER FIVE

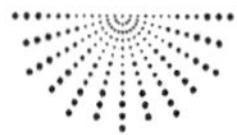

*L*ibby had fought back tears since Mark and Luke had dropped her off in the wee hours of the morning. She knew what she had to do and staying any longer would only make it harder.

Sleep had been impossible. As soon as the garage in Temptation had opened, she'd called Nick McBride, the owner and chief mechanic, asking him to collect her bike and make the necessary repairs. For the trip ahead, she also asked him to change the oil filter and give the machine a once-over for good measure.

Nick called two hours later, informing her that he'd replaced the cut fuel line and performed all the maintenance. The bike was ready to go.

Trouble was, Libby wasn't ready to leave Temptation. Not by a long shot. But she had to, or risk being found by her father and forced to return to a life she hated. The last place she'd stayed more than six months, her father had located her, his bodyguards surrounding her apartment building. If it had just been her father, she'd have risked seeing him. Maybe he'd listen this time to why she couldn't live with him anymore. It wasn't really her father that had made her run. It was the lifestyle he insisted she live.

Hell, sometimes she missed her father so much, it hurt. But she couldn't live in his ivory tower ever again. To avoid being trapped in that life, she'd had to leave without going back to collect her stuff. All she'd had when she'd arrived in Temptation was her bike and the clothes on her back.

Libby had walked the few blocks to the garage.

When she hadn't found Nick in the office, she stepped into the open bay, inhaling the strong scent of oil and grease, a strangely comforting smell reminding her of hard work and honest men.

Nick stood under a raised pickup, working a bolt loose with a wrench. Dressed in a grease-stained jumpsuit, he brushed at the sweat on his forehead, leaving a dark smear behind. Despite the sweat and grease, Nick was a handsome man and as friendly as the rest of the inhabitants of Temptation. She'd miss him. She hadn't trusted anyone with her beloved Beast as much as she trusted Nick. She'd miss a lot of people in the small town she'd called home for the past eight months.

Libby would miss Helen Roberts, the ancient cook at the Sweet Temptation Diner who always had a smile for her. And Calvin Northcutt, the old man who sat on the porch outside the General Store, greeting everyone who happened to walk by. She considered Kendall, Charli and Lacey, the waitresses at the saloon, her friends. They'd always included her on excursions to the malls in Austin, pizza parties, and even boating at the nearby lake. Libby always felt welcome, like one of the gals.

One of the hardest goodbyes, besides the Gray Wolf men, would be Audrey, the woman who'd offered her a job when Libby had been flat broke. She'd run out of gas on the county line at the end of the road where the Ugly Stick Saloon sat. Libby had stumbled into the saloon, looking for enough work to pay for a tank of gas and a sandwich. Audrey must have seen the desperation in Libby's eyes. She'd sat her down in the storeroom and brought her one of the sandwiches the saloon offered their customers. By the end of that night, Audrey had taken Libby under her wing and into her home, helping her get back on her feet. She'd been the sister Libby never had, the only family she claimed since she'd left New York City two years ago.

When she'd told Audrey she was leaving, her boss and friend had argued for an hour, trying to convince her to stay, to make Temptation her permanent home. Audrey had said she couldn't get along without Libby as the bartender, especially with the Cowboy Masquerade Ball coming up. But more than that, she couldn't imagine not having Libby around as a friend.

They'd ended up hugging. Libby had almost caved and told Audrey she'd stay forever. Especially now that she'd discovered what she'd pretty much known all along, and that was how wonderful Mark and Luke were.

But Libby couldn't stay and risk her father and his bodyguards catching up to her. She had to move on, or possibly lose the freedom and anonymity she treasured more than anything. Libby stood firm, telling Audrey she had to go, making one concession, promising to stay until after the Cowboy Masquerade Ball.

Audrey reluctantly agreed, promising not to say a word to the rest of the staff.

Now Libby stood outside the back door of the Ugly Stick Saloon, swallowing hard on the sobs rising up her throat. Mark and Luke had been there and left without so much as saying a word to her. She'd felt as if she'd been stabbed in the chest with a very sharp knife. It was all she could do to serve the men at the bar. Audrey had slipped up behind her with a bouquet of flowers, claiming the twins had left them for her and that she'd bet they were waiting outside, if Libby wanted to thank them. Audrey even offered to fill in for her behind the bar.

Glad to escape the noise and laughter inside, but nervous at the same time, Libby had dragged her feet on her way out the back door. Standing in the circle of light from the security lamp over the back door, she'd peered out into the darkness, unable to make out anyone. Perhaps Audrey had been wrong, and Mark and Luke had already left.

Libby sucked in a deep breath of the warm Texas air and stepped off the back stoop into the darkness, afraid they wouldn't be there, and even more afraid they would.

She hadn't taken ten steps, her eyes adjusting to the limited lighting, when two tall hulks loomed in front of her. Libby pressed a hand to her mouth, muffling a scream.

"Libby, it's us." Luke Gray Wolf touched her arm, his fingers warm and gentle against her skin.

She drew in a shaky breath. "You took a year off my life."

Mark smiled at her with a grin that melted Libby's knees. "Sorry. We thought you saw us."

Libby blinked up at him, her pulse leaping. "My eyes hadn't adjusted yet."

"You shouldn't walk out here alone." Luke's frown made her body warm. Obviously he cared about her safety.

But she didn't want him to care. She was leaving. Libby opened her mouth to say she could take care of herself.

Mark raised a hand to forestall her protest. "We know. You're a big girl. We just worry about you."

They wouldn't have to worry long. Once she was gone, they could move on with their lives, without Libby. Some lovely girls would snatch them up so fast, they'd never know what hit them. The thought of Mark and Luke with someone else made her stomach clench into a knot. She backed toward the door.

"You're right. I shouldn't be out here. I think I'll go back inside. I just came outside to thank you for the beautiful daisies."

Mark grinned. "The flowers were Luke's idea. Daisies were mine."

"You both did good. Daisies are my favorite." She gulped back a fresh sob and backed up another step. "Really, I'd better get back to work."

"Before you go…" Luke reached out and captured her hand. "We didn't hurt you last night, did we?"

She blinked hard to keep the tears from falling. "No. You didn't hurt me."

"Did my goofy brother offend you in any way?" Mark asked.

Luke punched him in the arm. "Hey."

Libby choked on what could barely be called a laugh. "No, you were both wonderful." That was the problem. She could very easily fall in love with them both…if she had more time.

"Then you're still coming on the ride with us tomorrow?" Luke lifted her hand to his lips and kissed the knuckles. "Please."

The look in his deep brown eyes melted a hole through her heart all the way into her soul. She couldn't afford to spend another minute alone with Mark and Luke, yet she couldn't reject them. "I don't know."

"She didn't say no." Mark swept her into his arms and planted a kiss on her lips.

"I didn't say yes," she reminded him breathlessly.

Luke gathered her close, his hands on either side of her cheeks. "We'll be waiting." Then he kissed her, his lips sliding over hers so gently, Libby's knees buckled. If he hadn't been holding her, she'd have melted to the ground. Biker-babe, huh! Pansy-ass, more like.

He set her away from him, tipped his hat and spun on his boot heels, striding away, reaching back to snag Mark's arm to drag him along with him. Within seconds, the two men were gone, leaving her standing in the gravel, her heart breaking into a million little pieces.

THAT NIGHT LUKE didn't sleep at all. After he'd pulled Mark away from Libby, he'd climbed in his truck and headed straight for the sheriff's office to have a talk with Jackson's buddy, Deputy Cramer, about what he might have found on Libby.

Which wasn't much. Unfortunately, or fortunately, no one by the name of Libby Jones had been reported missing in Texas or anywhere else in the nation.

"Next step is to check Libby's description against the nationwide database of missing persons. But that will have to wait until tomorrow." Deputy Cramer rose from behind his desk and stretched. "I'm beat, and unless you have more for me to go on, it could be a lengthy process."

Disappointment sank Luke's spirits. They knew so little about Libby. As the three men left the building, Luke remembered something Libby had said about not seeing the stars where she'd come from. He grabbed Cramer's arm before the man walked away. "Start with persons reported missing from New York City."

"That'll help narrow it down a little. Although New York City probably has its fair share of missing persons." Cramer waved. "I'll do that first thing."

Luke climbed into his truck and Mark slid into the passenger seat. With nothing more to go on, they were guaranteed a sleepless night, speculating on what made Libby want to skip town.

By five minutes after eleven o'clock the following day, Luke was so wound up he couldn't stand still. He'd flown through the regular chores, replaced a broken corral panel and answered several business calls, and still no sign of Libby.

He tossed a section of hay into the feed rack in the stall of their prized bay stallion, Bootlegger.

The horse nickered, tossing his glossy black mane as if sensing Luke's disquiet.

"Sorry, old man, can't take you out today. Diablo's coming and we want to impress the lady with our ability to maintain control, not lose it."

"Did you pack the chilled bottle of wine?" Mark called from outside the barn.

"Sure did." Luke led his gelding out of the barn and patted the saddlebag. He'd insisted on carrying the wine, not trusting Mark to get it there in one piece. "And I packed plastic wineglasses."

"Good." Mark rolled the brightly colored, woven Kiowa blanket and laid it over the back of his own saddlebag. "I have the sandwiches and chocolate strawberries. Women can't resist chocolate straw-berries."

"She may not even come." Luke shook his head, his gut clenching at the possibility.

"She'll come."

"How do you know?" He'd worried all night that she'd be a no-show.

"She didn't say no." Mark tied the saddlebag straps to his saddle and checked the tightness of the girth on his mount. "Damn, I forgot the suntan lotion." He turned toward the house, ready to run.

"Calm down. I got it. Good grief, Mark, why are you trying so hard? We've known Libby for almost eight months."

"This is the first time we've taken her out on a real date. Hell, it's only the second time she hasn't blown us off. And everything is riding on this day."

"Don't hang your hat on today." Luke's chest tightened. Libby was everything he'd ever dreamed of in a woman—smart, sexy, independent and beautiful. "No matter how hard we try, she might leave anyway."

Mark stared across at Luke. "No, we finally found a woman we're both crazy about and we've even agreed to share, we're not going to let her just walk away."

Luke wished Cramer had gotten back to them on his search of the missing persons' database, but so far, not a word. They'd be flying blind with Libby, relying solely on whatever bits of information she deigned to impart. "You know, I bet she's been burned before. We should treat her like a skittish colt. Gently. Give her a lot of space."

"I'd like to give her a lot more than space. You've

seen the way she moves, all sex and leather. Now that I know what's really under all that biker-girl getup, I can't get her out of my mind."

Luke had studied Libby over the past eight months, and Mark was right. Libby had a natural grace and beauty that no amount of leather leggings or tough-girl attitude could hide. "She's always acted like a badass, but based on last night, I'd say she's good at putting on a front. She's been hurt and she's afraid of being hurt again."

"Maybe so. It's up to us to show her that not all men are dickwads." Mark's face broke into a grin. "I told you she'd come."

The rumble of a motorcycle announced Libby's arrival. She rode up in a black leather jacket and matching chaps and gloves, her long, curly auburn hair streaming out from beneath the black helmet.

Mark tied off his horse and the one he'd selected for Libby and hurried forward to meet her.

"Remember what I said, Mark," Luke warned as Libby revved her engine one last time.

The three horses danced sideways, tugging against their leads.

Libby switched the key off, the engine noise ceased and the horses calmed. She pulled her helmet off and shook out her hair, her mirrored sunglasses hiding her eyes.

"My kind of woman—all sass and attitude." Mark reached for her helmet.

Luke's groin tightened, his thoughts echoing Mark's words. Damn, the woman looked incredibly dark and dangerous, sparking every nerve in his body to life, sending a rush of warm blood to one particular lower extremity.

She refused to let Mark take her helmet. "I'm not sure I'm staying."

"You came this far, you might as well." Luke stayed back, pretending indifference when he wanted to steal her key from her so that she couldn't take off.

She glanced at the three horses saddled and ready. "You two were pretty certain I'd show."

"Not certain…hopeful." Mark grinned and stepped toward his horse. "We have a picnic lunch, wine and a blanket. All we need is you and we're ready to go."

"Where?" she asked.

Luke smiled. "To see our special project."

Her brows rose. "You two have a special project?"

"Yes, ma'am, we do." Luke tipped his cowboy hat.

Libby's eyes narrowed and she chewed her bottom lip. "You know, the night before last was pretty spontaneous, and it was great and all, but it makes me wonder, do you always do everything together?"

Mark shrugged. "For the most part."

Her lips pressed together into a thin line. "Do you always share the same women?"

Libby's direct question made Luke wonder if their answer would convince her to stay or leave? He opted for the truth. "Not usually. Only if she's special."

"And, if she's willing and worth sharing." Mark glanced Luke. "We don't want to fight over anyone."

Luke nodded. They'd had their differences, but

they loved each other. "We agreed it's not worth losing a brother over."

Mark grinned. "We have to admit, sharing a woman between us keeps things interesting."

Libby's eyes were hidden by the sunglasses so Luke didn't have a hint as to what she was thinking, but a smile quirked the corners of her lips. "Speaking of sharing…I meant to ask the other night…was Audrey one of the women you shared?"

Broadsided by her question. Luke exchanged a look with Mark and then winked at Libby. "We don't kiss and tell."

Mark ducked his head, a smile sliding across his face.

For a long moment Libby remained seated on the motorcycle, her gaze running from Luke to Mark.

Luke swung up in his saddle and turned his horse around to face Libby, more nervous than he cared to admit, waiting for Libby to commit to coming, while thinking of ways to keep her from driving off should she decide not to. "Since you said you ride, I assume you know one end of the horse from the other. You know how to mount?"

Libby sucked in a deep breath and let it out, then swung her leg over the bike seat. "I do." She laid her helmet on the back of the motorcycle, removed her sunglasses, tucking them into the helmet, and then walked toward him.

The knot in Luke's gut loosened and he fought to keep from smiling.

"Want me to give you a leg up?" Mark brought

forward the bay mare they'd selected for Libby to ride.

"No thanks. I like doing things on my own," she said, her voice edgy.

Mark handed her the reins. "This is Jezebel, one of the mares we use for breeding stock. She's a good, solid ride, no surprises."

"She's beautiful." Libby smoothed her hand over the animal, lifting the stirrup to check the tightness of the girth. Then she slipped the reins over the mare's neck and patted her flanks, speaking soothingly as she placed her black boot into the left stirrup and floated up into the saddle like it was second nature to her. She sat tall, her back poker straight, the reins in separate hands like someone used to riding English-style.

"'Round here, we ride western-style—reins together." Luke held up his reins in one hand. "Jezebel responds to the lightest movement of the straps over her neck."

Placing both reins in one hand, Libby tugged the pair to the left. Jezebel turned left. She performed the same instruction going right, then nodded to Luke. "Ready?"

"Ready," he answered and led off at a walk.

Mark unlatched the gate for them, opening out into the pasture stretching to the west across pastures of second-growth new hay only a foot deep and as green as an emerald blanket.

Luke led the way through, waiting for Libby and Mark to come abreast.

Then he set the pace at an easy, smooth canter,

suddenly anxious to show Libby what he and his brother had been working on. He hoped she liked it.

The sun shone down from a bright, summer sky filled with puffy white clouds. The land stretched before them over rolling hills. As they rode to the top of each rise, they could see all around, not a house, person or car in sight besides the three of them. Luke and Mark had chosen the location of their project because it was far off the beaten path. Sure, they could drive in from the road, and they did when they had to bring in lumber and supplies, but Luke had wanted to take the horses to show Libby that riding horses could be just as open and free as riding the open road on a motorcycle. Even more so.

They rode in silence, down into green valleys, wading through sparkling brooks and up over the tops of ridges. When they came to the grasslands surrounding a particularly tall hill, Luke glanced over at Libby. "Up for a little race?"

Her eyes narrowed. "Question is, are you?"

He nodded. "To the top of the hill."

Before the last word left Luke's lips, Libby dug her heels into the mare's flanks. The horse leaped forward, galloping across a wide swath of lush green grass.

Mark, riding Diablo, the black stallion who'd sired many of the horses the ranch was known for, took the lead, the horse's long neck stretching forward.

Luke's gelding strained to catch up to the mare, settling into a steady gallop alongside. Luke purposely held his mount back to allow Libby to reach the top at the same time as he did.

Libby bent over her mare, almost touching her neck, her eyes narrowed, lips set in a firm line of concentration. When they topped the hill, Libby pulled back on the reins, laughing, her burnished copper hair tangled, her face flushed, and her green eyes glistening in the bright Texas sun.

Luke's breath caught in his throat. Damn, the woman was even more beautiful in natural lighting than in the darker interior of the Ugly Stick Saloon. And she'd come out to play with them. His groin tightened and his hands squeezed the reins as he prayed he and his brother could somehow convince her to stay.

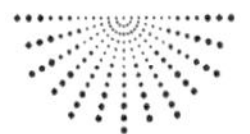

With a whoop, Libby spun her horse around and waited for the two men to join her.

The rush of air in her face, the speed of her ascent up the hill and the view when she arrived took her breath away. The land slipped down and away from the hill with a three-hundred-sixty degree view of sky that went on forever, not a single building, person or vehicle within sight, except for the shell of what looked like a future home crowning the hilltop. It was a perfect location, away from it all. For a brief moment Libby wished it could be hers.

A gentle breeze stirred tendrils of hair against her cheeks. She'd been many places on the back of her Harley and in her other life, traveling with her family, but never had she seen anywhere as isolated and peaceful. She felt as if she stood at the edge of the world, a launching point in which she could choose any direction.

"What do you think of our project?" Luke asked.

Libby had barely noticed when the other two horses had joined hers. Nor had she been aware the men had dismounted. Her chest swelled, her heart hammering against her ribs. "Beautiful."

"Yes, you are." Luke stood beside her, reaching up his hands, capturing her around her waist.

Stunned by the splendor around her, she didn't resist when he swung her down out of the saddle and onto her feet. Nor did she squawk when he pressed a kiss to her forehead. "Your eyes are shining. I take it you like our little corner of heaven." As quickly as he'd kissed her, he set her away, putting distance between them.

Libby marveled that she hadn't had the urge to run. Having Luke hold her close and kiss her didn't make her squirm and want to push away. In New York City, she'd been labeled the Debutante Ice Queen. So many men saw her as a challenge, sure that they could win her heart and tap into her father's riches, when all she wanted was to be left alone.

Not so with Luke and Mark. They seemed to instinctively know when to hold her and when to let her go.

With so much sunshine and sky around her, she felt as if she were perched on a cloud.

Because the men seemed to be anxiously awaiting her verdict on their building, she turned her attention to the house.

Built of timber and glass, the one-story home appeared to have light streaming in, through and around it, with no apparent solid walls on the outside. A wooden deck surrounded all four sides and the structure was capped by a roof with skylights almost as frequent as the solar panels positioned to collect the abundant source of the sky's energy.

Libby moved toward the house. "Is this one of your construction projects?" She'd known they were both in construction, one the builder, the other the designer. From what Audrey had said, they did well as a team, making a living even in tough economic times because of their ingenious designs and quality.

Mark hurried ahead of her, taking the steps two at a time up onto the deck, carrying a saddlebag and a rolled-up blanket. "We started it about four months ago, and should finish in another two."

She climbed the wide wooden steps to the deck that was absent of any wooden railing, adding to the effect of openness and freedom. "It's beautiful here and…so quiet."

Luke stood beside her, staring out at the land and sky. "We like to come here to get away from the noise."

"Really?" She rolled her eyes. "I see you at the Ugly Stick often enough, making some of that noise."

"See? She does notice us." Mark grinned at Luke. "We like to make noise when we like to, but when the day is done, we come out here for the peace."

Luke stared out over the land. "It's where we do our best thinking."

"I can see why. It's remarkable." Libby gazed at the landscape, one hand resting over her heart, her chest filling with a huge sense of coming home. She tried to push it back, but the sensation wouldn't abate and it scared her.

"We call it Skyview." Luke smiled. "We don't need fancy pictures on the walls, nature is the best artwork we've discovered."

Mark stood on her other side, still holding the blanket, having slung his saddlebag over his shoulder. "Hungry?"

"A little." Libby was surprised at how hungry she was. Because she'd been so upset by her pending move, she hadn't been able to eat all day yesterday nor that morning. The ride out, the open air and sunshine must have been doing her some good, resurrecting her appetite.

Having lived in Temptation, Texas for eight months was making her antsy, impatient, fearful, and aware it was about time to move on or be discovered.

For two years, she'd been moving from town to town, never staying more than a few months, just long enough to make a few bucks to pay for gas to get her to the next town. But something about the Ugly Stick Saloon and Audrey had appealed to her, making her want to stay a little longer than usual. Audrey had a way of collecting strays. Not that Libby considered herself a stray. She hadn't been looking for a home, just a temporary stop on her journey across the country.

"Can I see the inside of the house first?" she asked as she stared through the huge windows.

Luke led the way, room to room. From a gleaming stainless steel kitchen to the living room that took up all of one side of the house, she had a view through floor-to-ceiling windows.

Even the bedrooms had glass windows with a view as stunning as the opposite side of the house.

Besides the living room, Libby counted four spacious rooms that could be bedrooms and a study with two desks. "You two are really planning to live here together?"

Mark nodded. "We'd considered building two houses, but why waste space? We're together all the time."

She stared at the twins. "Don't you get tired of each other?"

Mark and Luke looked at each other and shook their heads.

"No," Luke answered. "We know how the other thinks and what sets each other off. You could say we're pretty much in sync."

"What about curtains for the bedrooms?" She nodded toward the windows.

Mark grinned. "We'll have shades that can be drawn when the sun is too hot coming through. But frankly, we're in no hurry. Since there are no neighbors close enough to peek in, it isn't an issue."

Luke stared out at the horizon. "We like how open it is."

Libby nodded and whispered, "Me, too."

"It'll be like making love in the open air," Mark stated. "There's nothing sexier."

A flush of heat washed over Libby's body at the memory of making love with these men under the Texas sky filled with a millions of sparkling stars. The surge of desire was proof, yet again, that her family hadn't totally killed the exhibitionist inside of her. Her belly tightened and a rush of moisture pooled between her legs. *Oy vey*, the twins were making her hotter than she'd ever imagined possible. She shouldn't have waited two years to act on her sexual desires. Come to think of it, she hadn't been tempted in those two years until she'd seen Luke and Mark on the dance floor of the Ugly Stick Saloon. And she probably wouldn't have acted on those desires had she decided to stay. Sex complicated things.

"You'll have to come sometime when a storm rolls in." Mark broke into her steamy thoughts. "It's incredible."

Libby pulled her mind out of the bedroom and let out a shaky breath. "I bet."

The house was different from the high-rise apartment she'd lived in most of her life in Manhattan, surrounded by concrete, steel, millions of people and her father's bodyguards and security system. In comparison, this place was truly a slice of heaven. She could love living here, if her life was her own. But it wasn't until she was truly free and she'd never be truly free from her father's notoriety and the paparazzi.

Her shoulders straightened. "You said you have food?"

Mark laughed. "We do, come on." He hurried out of the house.

Libby hesitated, enjoying the light coming through the windows and the way the clouds looked close enough to touch.

Luke stood beside her. "He planned this whole picnic just for you."

Through the window, Libby could see Mark shaking the blanket out on the deck and removing items from the saddlebags, laying them out one at a time. The blanket's corners flipped up in the breeze.

"Why me?" she asked.

"Seriously?" Luke took her arms and stared down into her eyes. "You're beautiful, you love to ride and could probably kick our asses if you took a mind to." He kissed the tip of her nose. "Mark and I have wanted you for a very long time."

Her brows dipped. "Yeah? And dancing with every girl in the bar is your way of showing me that?"

Luke shrugged. "We love music and dancing. What can I say? It makes us happy. But after the other night…we can't imagine anyone else in our lives but you."

Libby stared up at him for a moment, the light in his dark eyes making her sway closer, drawing her to him like a snake to a charmer.

"You two coming?" Mark leaned in the doorway, his brows furrowing as he spotted them.

Heat rushed up her throat into her cheeks and Libby pushed away from Luke. "I'm coming."

"Good. I'd hate for the two of you to start without me." Mark held the door for her. As she passed through, he swatted her on the fanny.

"Hey! What was that for?" Libby rubbed where he'd touched her, the image of lying with the twins under the stars returning in full force. Between Luke's deep, serious looks and Mark's playful pats, she was well on her way to being all hot and bothered again by these men. Perhaps being alone with them hadn't been such a good idea.

Then why was she anticipating their next move, hoping to recreate the magic of a starry Texas night?

Mark laid the saddlebags on two of the corners of the blanket to hold them down and set a bottle of wine in the middle, complete with three plastic wineglasses, which he promptly filled.

He handed one to Libby, one to Luke and took the third for himself. "Here's to getting to know all about you."

Libby hesitated, her hand trembling for a second before she steadied it. "You know how I am about questions. How about toasting to freedom?"

"Fair enough." Mark threw back his head, swallowing the wine in his glass in one gulp. "But Luke and I do want to get to know you better."

"Maybe after lunch." Libby reached for a sandwich wrapped in cellophane. "I'm starving."

From the corner of her eye, she could see Luke

frowning at his brother, giving him a slight shake of his head, using their silent twin communication.

They sat on the blanket, their long legs stretching out on both sides of her, broad shoulders filling the space around her. If not for the open sky and the view from the hilltop, she might have felt hemmed in, trapped. But the setting couldn't have been more perfect.

When they'd finished the sandwiches, Mark moved the glasses, bottle and wrappers to the side, unbuttoned his shirt and shrugged it off. He tossed it to the side, then laid back on the blanket.

Libby's heart sputtered as she stared at Mark's smooth chest, her core clenching at all the lovely naked, dark skin covering thick, well-defined muscles she'd seen only in the moonlight. "What are you doing?"

Mark blinked. "I'm sorry, I should have asked. Luke and I always take off our shirts when we're out here. Especially when it gets warm like it is today." He reached for his shirt. "I can put it back on if you like."

"No, no, that's fine." Heat filled her cheeks and parts farther south. "Only seems natural out here."

"In that case…" Luke stripped his shirt and tossed it to the side, lying back on the blanket just like his brother. "Mark and I like to come out here after dark. Just like the place we took you to the other night, there are so few lights around, you can see all the stars in the sky."

Libby lay on the blanket between them, her pulse

beating faster than it should for someone in a resting position, unless that someone was being made love to.

The thought slipped in before Libby could block it and her core bloomed with warmth. What would it hurt to make love to these men one more time? She was free, wasn't she? Capable of making her own decisions, not accountable to anyone but herself.

Why was she holding back, when all she wanted was to toss off her clothes and go at it like a rabbit in heat? She moaned.

"Are you all right?" Luke propped up on an elbow, his brows furrowing.

Mark did the same. "Did lunch not agree with you?"

"No, I'm fine," she lied. Fine by whose standards? Except for the night before last, the only sex she'd had for the past two years had been with her trusty vibrator. "What is it you two treated Audrey to that she saw fit to tease me about without telling?"

Mark smiled. "She was the one who treated the three of us."

Libby's brows rose. "I didn't get that impression."

Luke traced a finger along her side. "Did she tell you that she danced for all three of us?"

"Yeah. And she was hot in those red boots and the chaps." Mark whistled. "Jackson's one lucky son of a gun."

Libby's brows furrowed, her gut tightening with a touch of jealousy. "Is that what it takes to turn you guys on, boots and chaps?"

Mark's brows rose into the dark black hair

hanging down into his eyes. "You know better than that. Didn't the night before last prove it?"

"Oh, sweetheart." Luke chuckled, the sound spreading over Libby like melted chocolate. "It only takes a smile to turn on my brother."

"What about you?" Libby asked Luke.

His smile straightened. "A smart woman, a little skin and encouragement."

"Is that all?" Her insides flamed at the way Luke's gaze ran down her fully clothed length. Her heart galloping in her chest, Libby made up her mind. With a deep breath, she sat up, pulled her T-shirt over her head and tossed it aside with Mark and Luke's shirts and lay down with a smile, closing her eyes to the brightness of the sun. She waited for her invitation to be accepted.

And waited…and waited.

Finally she opened her eyes and stared up at Mark and Luke. They were grinning down at her.

Luke spoke first. "Why did you come out here today, Libby?"

Libby frowned, her face burning. "Sorry, I thought you two were interested in sex. My mistake." She sat up and leaned across Mark, reaching for her shirt.

As her bare skin connected with his, her pussy creamed and she fought to drag air into her lungs. How embarrassing to be so brazen with these two men and them not want any part of her.

Mark's arms wrapped around her, dragging her up his body to face him. "I don't make it a habit to pounce on a woman, unless I know for certain that's what she wants. Up until the point you took off your shirt, I wasn't hedging my bets."

"And he wanted to pounce." Luke laughed. "My brother isn't known for his willpower when it comes to a beautiful woman."

Still stinging from their lack of response, Libby pushed against Mark's chest, her fingers meeting with the hard muscles. "I took off my shirt. Good grief, what did you think I meant?"

"After the other night, we're not sure what *you* want, but we know what we want. We want you." Luke shook his head, a smile lifting the corners of his lips. "Still, considering your decision to leave town after what we'd shared the other night, we weren't going to risk making any assumptions. If you want to make love with us, say so."

Oh, man, she wanted to really bad, her entire body tensed with frustration. "That's what I *wanted*." She stretched her arm farther, her fingers grasping for the shirt she hoped to hide behind. "Now, I'm just embarrassed."

Luke moved closer, his hand smoothing across her back, scraping over her bra. "Just so you know, ever since we made this arrangement, I for one, haven't been able to stop thinking about you and what you might look like beneath the biker-chick outfit in broad daylight."

Libby's breath caught and her struggle to grab her shirt ceased. "And?"

"And I like the leather and attitude, and I like

making love in the starlight, but I like this better." Luke's fingers spread wide across her lower back, smoothing over her black jeans and pulling at the straps to loosen her black leather chaps. "You are beautiful."

"Now I can see the sunlight on your hair and the deep green of your eyes." Mark dug his hands into her hair, pulling her closer to press his lips to hers.

While Luke slipped her chaps out from between her and Mark, Mark plunged his tongue between Libby's teeth, stroking the length of hers in long, lazy thrusts.

Libby's fingers dug into Mark's chest, her legs parting over his hips.

The handsome Kiowa pressed the swell of his cock against her pussy through his jeans, inspiring all kinds of crazy, kinky thoughts to go flitting through her head.

Lying in the open air, with nothing nearby but sky and miles of open country, far away from prying eyes, her breathing grew ragged.

Luke slid his fingers along her spine, up to where her bra pressed against her ribs. "I'd personally like to see a little more."

Breaking free of Mark's soul-stealing kiss, Libby sat up, grinding her cunt against the ridge of his fly. "Look, guys. I'm here for the sex. Nothing else. No tomorrows, no commitment. Got that?"

Mark held his hands up in surrender, his face strained, his cock swelling beneath her. "Got it. For now. Could you shift just a little to the left?"

Luke frowned. "What if we want to see you tomorrow?"

Her belly clenched. She didn't have tomorrows she could give to anyone. Knowing she'd stayed too long already made her more determined to grab a little joy out of the moment. With a sigh, she answered, "No guarantees. I may not be around. This offer is only good for today. And it expires in one minute. The time it'll take me to change my mind."

Mark moaned. "I'm in."

"I'm not so sure I am." Luke bent and pressed a kiss to the tip of one breast. "I can't imagine this being the last time with you."

"It might be all I have to give," she said.

"Then let's make it good, so she'll *want* to come back." Mark's face had reddened and his hands clamped on Libby's hips, rubbing her against him. "For crissakes, Luke, don't analyze everything to death. She wants uncommitted sex. Let's give the lady what she wants."

Libby's shoulders pushed back, her breasts bobbing free. The expression on Luke's face, those intense brown eyes, nearly had her begging.

Finally, he nodded. "Okay. No strings. No tomorrows. But I plan on making today last as long as possible."

She held out her hand and shook his. Where he gripped her fingers, they tingled, sending little electric shocks straight south to that wet, pulsing place that needed them now. "Deal."

Mark pushed her to a standing position and

leaped out from under her, popping the top button on his jeans.

Luke frowned. "Geez, Mark, have a little couth."

His brother groaned and jerked the other three buttons of his jeans loose in one movement. His cock sprang free, hard and straight, fully engorged. Mark sagged in relief. "Next time you decide to have a conversation with her, do it when her pussy isn't rubbing my dick."

Libby glanced at Mark's cock, her tongue sweeping across suddenly dry lips. "Oh my, in the light of day, I see what Audrey was talking about."

"You haven't seen anything yet," Luke promised.

Mark laughed. "Quit braggin' and show her whatcha got, bro."

"First things first." On his knees on the blanket, Luke reached for the button on Libby's jeans, flicking the rivet through the hole. As he slid the zipper down, his fingers followed, sliding beneath her black, lace panties.

Mark kicked off his boots and shucked his jeans, flinging them off the deck entirely, standing naked and magnificent in all his Native American glory. Naturally tanned skin stretched taut over his entire body. His smooth, hairless, muscular chest rippled with every movement.

Libby couldn't drag her gaze away from where his waist narrowed to tight hips and that enormous cock jutted fiercely in front of him. *Oh, my.*

Then Luke's hands pushed her jeans down over her thighs, his fingers blazing a trail across her skin.

He lifted one of her feet, untied the black biker boot and pulled it free, taking the jean leg with it.

Mark stepped up in front of Libby to steady her as Luke stripped her body of every stitch, leaving the black lace panties for last.

Standing in the warm sun, her fair skin tingling, Libby reached for the elastic waistband of her panties, anxious now to be completely free of all constrictions.

Luke's hand covered hers, stopping her from removing the last barrier. "Wait. I want to be as naked as you two before we move on."

Libby turned to face Luke.

He stood, reaching for his waistband.

She pushed his hands to the side and slipped her fingers beneath the waistband of his jeans, fingering the top button. "You take entirely too long. Let me."

Mark groaned behind her, pressing his cock against her bottom. "I tried to tell him that, but he insists on taking it slowly with you."

"Do you take it slowly with your other women?" she asked.

"As far as I'm concerned, there are no other women." Luke's hands dropped to his sides, allowing her to take charge.

Libby snorted. "Right." She glanced over her shoulder. "Mark?"

"No. We get right down to business."

Luke glared at his brother. "I told you…Libby is different."

"And she wants sex. Don't stand in the way of her

getting what she wants. Ol' Pleaze can tell you that's not a good idea."

Libby shook her head, her hands still resting on the top button of Luke's jeans. "I promise not to hurt either one of you."

"I doubt you'll keep that promise," Luke said softly.

Her brows furrowed. "I keep my promises."

"Okay, okay." Luke's hands rose to cup her arms, urging her to continue undressing him. "Then let Mark and I remind you what it's like with two men."

"About time." She flicked the first button loose and yanked the remaining buttons free of their holes. His cock jutted forward into her palm.

"You two are physically identical in every way." Her eyes rounded and her breathing grew ragged as her pussy creamed, pulsing in anticipation of having both of them inside her. "I never knew how good it could be, two men at once. I believe I'm ruined for anything else," she whispered, her hand gliding over Luke's length. She reached back to capture Mark's dick in her hand, holding both, lingering over the velvety smooth skin stretched over steel rods.

Luke hooked her panties and slid them down her legs to her ankles. As he rose in front of her, his hand cupped her pussy, his fingers sliding deep into her.

Libby's head fell back, a moan rising from deep inside, escaping into the open air.

Mark's hands cupped her breasts from behind. "Sweetheart, let us show you how good it can be in the daylight."

# CHAPTER SEVEN

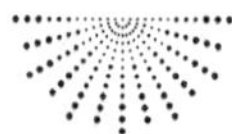

Mark flinched when she tightened her grip on his cock. Her warm hand on his shaft felt so damned good, he had to grit his teeth. "At this rate, I'll come before we even get started."

"You're such a teenager, Mark," Luke scolded. "How many times have I told you that women like foreplay?"

"Screw foreplay." Libby's hand squeezed Mark's cock. "Hell, I'm dripping. You should know." She moved her legs wider apart, pressing Luke's fingers deeper. "As long as you have protection, I'm ready."

Mark made a dive off the deck for the jeans he'd tossed, coming up with his wallet and an accordion of condoms. "Is this enough?"

She laughed. "It'll do for a start."

The promise of more than once that day was enough to make Mark shoot his wad, but he held on, his dick aching for release. He tore off one packet and

"Oh, my." She squirmed.

Luke's fingers slipped between Libby and Mark, circling her pussy and Mark's cock, gathering enough moisture to lubricate her anus.

The sensation of Libby's muscles tightening around his cock sent tiny electric shocks across Mark's nerve endings and he withdrew again, then slid back in. Once, twice and then he pulled out.

Luke slid free as well.

"Why are you stopping?" Libby wailed, still clinging to his waist with her legs.

"We have so much more we want to do with you, we don't want to waste it all on one ejaculation." Mark set her on her feet and stripped the rubber off.

Luke peeled off his condom, tipped his head toward his brother and grinned. "Show her how to ride."

Mark lifted Libby up in his arms and carried her down the steps of the deck, then set her on her saddle.

"We're not going back yet, are we?" She wrapped her arms across her breasts. "Especially not naked."

Mark shook his head. "Not yet." He swung up on the back of the horse and scooted into the saddle, lifting her and settling her on his lap, facing him, his unsheathed cock sliding into her.

"Okkaayay," she said, the air whooshing out of her. "Another first for me."

"We're safe and I promise not to come inside you."

"I'm safe too, and on the pill, if that makes a difference."

Mark grinned. "Hot damn! It feels so good to be

skin-to-skin. You have to admit, this brings riding to a whole other level." Mark took up the reins and nudged the horse, sending it at a sedate pace down the hill toward a wooded valley.

Luke mounted his horse behind them, his dick still just as stiff and straight as it had been.

Libby swayed with the motion of the horse, Mark's cock buried inside her, her arms resting on his shoulders, the tips of her breasts peaked and touching his magnificent chest.

"Do you like this?" he asked.

"Ummm, yes. And to think I've been riding horses most of my life and never once did I do this. I'll never be able to ride normal again."

"You will." Mark bent to take a nipple between his teeth, rolling the nub around before laving it with his tongue. As his head came up, he captured her lips with his, kissing her until she was breathless.

The horse had come to a halt by the time the kiss ended.

Luke stood on the ground, naked and horny, based on the size of his member. He held his hands up for Libby. "Come on, you'll like this."

Mark eased her off his cock and she leaned down into his brother's arms.

LUKE SCOOPED an arm beneath her legs and carried her down the embankment and right into a cool, clear pool of water, going deeper and deeper until he stood waist deep and Libby's bottom dipped beneath the surface.

"You can let go of me," she said. "I know how to swim."

Luke let her feet drop to the sandy bottom, cupped her face in his hands and kissed her. "Swim."

He struck out, aiming for a trickling waterfall at the opposite end of the pool, ducking beneath the water, willing his cock to shrink a little before they started to pleasure her again.

Something caught his ankle and he was dragged under. When he surfaced, Libby was laughing, standing on her toes to keep her head above the water. She pushed off the bottom and floated on her back, staring up at the sky. "This place is magical. Everywhere I look, I can see the sky."

"We like it." Luke stood beside her in the water, giving up on willing his swelled dick down. He wanted to drive into her, to fuck her until he exploded in a burst of ecstasy. He held her steady in front of him, his hand under her back. Then he leaned over and pinched the tip of one pointed breast.

She moaned. "Do that again."

Mark floated up to where Libby lay on her back in the water and slipped his hands beneath her shoulders.

Luke parted her legs and slipped between them, holding her ass up out of the water so that he could taste her in her most sensitive place. He trailed a line of kisses and nips up her inner thigh.

She wiggled, her knees draping over his shoulders, bending to give him better access.

His tongue touched her entrance, licking her, tasting her essence. Then he dove in, swirling inside as far as his tongue could reach.

She reached between her legs, digging her fingers into his hair, holding him close, her pelvis rocking upward. "Please."

Luke moved up, parting her folds and tonguing her clit, laving the sweet, tender flesh until she cried out, her body bucking in the water.

"I want you inside me. Now!" she cried, wiggling out of Luke and Mark's hold, her feet sinking below the surface. She wrapped her legs around Luke and sank down over his cock.

Mark pressed against her back, his hands coming between her and Luke, holding her breasts, tweaking the tips of her nipples.

Luke drove into her as he pressed her down over his member. He pumped in and out of her until the tension built to a peak and he shot over the edge. Holding her hips steady, he thrust into her one last time, his penis throbbing, the ache so beautiful he didn't want to let go.

Libby lay back against Mark, her eyes open, staring up at the blue sky, her mouth curved into a smile. "So much better than my vibrator."

Mark laughed out loud.

Luke eased out of Libby and let her feet drop down. "Come on, let's get some of that sunshine you seem to like so much."

THEY SWAM to a nearby rock ledge that hung out over the pool. Mark lifted Libby up onto the ledge and climbed up next to her. Luke ducked under water and surfaced shaking out his long dark hair.

Libby laughed as she was covered in spray. Then she lay back on the rock, the sun warming her skin through the opening in the canopy of trees above. "You can do this every day?"

"When we're not working." Luke hiked himself up onto the rock and lay on the other side of Libby.

Libby sighed, her smile slipping from her face. "You could almost hide from the world out here."

"If we wanted." Mark leaned up on his side, propping his cheek on his elbow. "Freedom means a lot to you, doesn't it?"

She nodded, refusing to go into the details of her former life. The less anyone knew, the less of a chance they'd find her.

Luke leaned up on his elbow, glistening drops of water sliding down over his dark, magnificent chest. "Not going to tell us anything about who Libby is, are you?"

"No. Talk is overrated." Libby reached out and traced a rivulet down to his waist, admiring his rock-hard abs and the now flaccid cock, still bigger than most even in the dormant state. She touched it.

Luke's stomach muscles clenched and his cock swelled. "I could go again, if that's what you want."

Mark cleared his throat. "I'm still hard, no work involved here."

Libby leaned up on both elbows, her gaze going

from one cock to the other, her tongue snaking out across her bottom lip as she recalled how sexy Mark had tasted inside her mouth.

Mark was right, he was engorged, his rod thick and hard.

That familiar ache built low in Libby's belly, her pussy gushing at the thought of taking Mark into her mouth. She pushed him to lie flat on his back, leaned over him and licked the tip of his penis, then traced the rim of his head, her tongue rising over the smooth cone to dip into the hole already oozing come.

"Umm. My turn to relieve you."

She rose up on her knees, cool air brushing across her sensitized ass and, as she bent to wrap her hands around his dick, the breeze swept across her heated pussy, reminding her of how decadent it was to be out in nature, naked and completely free of the trappings of society. Libby cupped Mark's balls, rolling them between her fingers as she opened her mouth and slid down over him.

Mark's hips thrust upward, his cock filling her mouth, bumping into the back of her throat. She flicked his head with the tip of her tongue and slid off.

Hands caressed her ass, one reaching between her legs to cup her pussy. She moved her knees farther apart, allowing Luke better access.

As she moved her head up and down over Mark's dick, increasing the speed to match his thrusts, Luke slid a finger into her pussy, pumping in and out, then he pushed a finger into her ass.

On fire, with the taste of Mark's cock in her

mouth and Luke's fingers thrusting in and out of her, Libby's muscles tensed, her back arching, a moan rising from her throat.

Beneath her hands, Mark's hips rocked again and again, thrusting his cock upward until he froze, his muscles hard, his dick harder. He pulled out of her mouth as come shot out, spewing over Libby's chin and down her neck.

Mark scooted under her and took a nipple in his mouth, sucking hard, while his fingers sought her folds, parting them to find that sensitive bud, soft, moist and swollen, and he stroked.

Libby's insides bunched, tingles starting in her toes and spreading like wildfire throughout her body.

Luke removed his fingers from her and thrust his now hard cock into her pussy.

With Mark on her clit and Luke inside, Libby rocketed to the moon, crying out as her orgasm shook her. Wave after wave of ecstasy washed over her until she thought she might completely come apart.

Luke tensed, his body going rigid, then he pulled free, come spilling across the rock.

When her body quit spasming, Libby spread out on the rock, staring up at the sky, unable to speak, not wanting to, and perfectly content to stay right where she was forever.

Mark trailed a hand over her breast, Luke skimmed her belly with his fingers, moving lower to thread through the tuft of hair over her mons.

"That was great," she whispered. "Audrey was

right. You two are amazing."

"Only with the right woman," Luke said.

"With you," Mark agreed.

"And you don't have to be back at work until tomorrow night." Mark stared down at her, a smile curling the corners of his lips. "Wait until you see what else this dog and pony show can do."

"After that, you'll never want to leave."

A pang of regret threatened to suck away Libby's sunshine. "You two don't know how lucky you have it out here."

Mark looked at Luke and they both laughed. "Oh, yes we do. We have the earth, the sky and a beautiful woman. What more could we ask for?"

"I've never felt more free and peaceful than I've felt here, with you two." Libby sighed and reached for them. *If only it could last.*

But Luke and Mark wouldn't let her slide into a funk.

True to their words, they showed her the best time a girl could have. For the rest of Thursday and into Friday morning, she never heard a phone ring, or saw a car or another human besides Mark and Luke. Libby remained naked, fucked and completely sexually sated.

Life didn't get better than that.

Her one regret…she'd have to wake up someday. She couldn't stay forever.

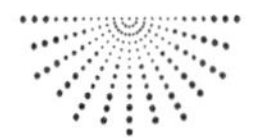

# CHAPTER EIGHT

"I told you, didn't I?" Audrey pulled Libby into the storeroom as soon as she showed up for work on Friday, an hour late and walking a little funny. "They were unbelievable, weren't they?"

Even riding her bike back from the Gray Wolf Ranch had been a challenge. Every time she shifted on the seat, the raw and sensitive areas around her pussy sent shock waves throughout her body, making her almost come just driving to work. She was breathing hard and fast by the time she pulled into the parking lot and shut off her bike.

Making the trek into the building had been slow and deliciously painful, every step a reminder of all the times she'd made love with the two men. A woman couldn't possibly get bored when she had two men to keep her entertained in bed...or on a rock...a deck…in a secluded pool, the yard, the kitchen counter.

Her face heated as she stood in front of her boss. The experience was too new, too erotic for her to share so soon. Hell, she could barely process it herself, much less report on her antics to Audrey. Libby forced a nonchalant shrug. "They were okay."

Audrey laughed out loud. "Liar. If they were anything like they'd been with me and Jackson, they were freakin' awesome. And you've had them all to yourself for twenty-four hours?" Her boss sighed. "If Jackson wasn't more man than I can handle by myself, I might be a little jealous." She grabbed Libby and hugged her tight. "When are you seeing them again?"

She missed them already, and it scared her more than she could say. Libby stepped back and turned away. "I won't be seeing them again."

Audrey snagged her elbow and spun her back to face her. "What? You have to. I've never seen you so wonderfully off-balance. It's bound to be doing you a world of good to let your guard down and relax for once."

"You don't understand, Audrey, I can't let my guard down." Tears pooled in Libby's eyes. "I can't."

Audrey held her at arm's length. "Why, sweetie? The Gray Wolfs won't hurt you."

"It's not them." She caught herself before blurting out the truth. "I refuse to give up my freedom. I've worked too hard to maintain it for the past two years."

"What are you talking about? Who's trying to take away your freedom?" Audrey stared hard into her eyes. "Tell me, Libby. Are you in trouble with the law? Maybe I can help."

For an achingly long moment, Libby considered sharing her secret with her friend. But sharing only exposed her and she couldn't let them find her. "I've already been here too long," Libby whispered. She hugged Audrey and stepped out of her arms. "I've told you, I have to leave. I promised to stay through the Cowboy Masquerade Ball. After tonight, that's it. I'm leaving."

Audrey's eyes opened wide, her arms crossing over her chest. "What did those two do to you?"

Libby laughed through her tears. "Only the most wonderful things a girl could imagine. But I can't stay. Like I said, I've already stayed too long."

"Baby, I can't afford to lose you." Audrey hugged her. "You're the best darned bartender I've ever had. No one can flip a bottle or dance like you."

Libby smiled. "You can. And you don't need me. You have Kendall, Lacey and Charli and the new girl, Bella. They're all wonderful."

"But why?" Audrey's eyes filled. "Was it something I said?"

"No, you've been the best, and I'll hate leaving you and all my friends." *And the Gray Wolf men*, she didn't say out loud. But she'd miss them as well. Too bad she hadn't discovered their delights earlier on in her stay in Temptation. But that was part of keeping a low profile, staying out of the public eye, and forming no attachments.

When Audrey opened her mouth to say something else, Libby lifted a hand.

"Please, Audrey. I have to leave. I don't have any other choice. Don't make it harder than it already is."

Audrey nodded. "Okay, but I don't like it, and I'm going to miss you like all get-out. Damn it, girl." She hugged her again. "Will you at least work through tonight's Cowboy Masquerade Ball and the next two nights of the rodeo? I need everyone who can work to be here this weekend. You know how busy we get."

Libby shook her head. "I'm sorry. I'll work tonight, but then I'm gone."

Audrey wiped a tear from the corner of her eye. "You'll always be welcome back at the Ugly Stick Saloon, you know that?"

Libby smiled. "I know. Thank you for taking in this stray when I needed it."

"Best stray I've ever adopted. Don't stay away long. I already miss you."

Libby dashed away the tears that had spilled over and sniffed. "I'd better get to work. The early birds will be yammerin' for their beer."

"Yeah." Audrey wiped more tears from her eyes.

Libby turned toward the bar, her feet dragging, her heart heavy.

"Hey, wait, Libby. I almost forgot. The girls are all wearing matching costumes so the patrons will know who's working here, and don't forget we're dancing on the bar tonight. One more show for the road, huh?" Audrey dashed into the storeroom and returned with a bright red corset and a red and black flounce skirt. "This should fit you."

Libby's mouth dropped open. As part of the hiring requirements for working at the Ugly Stick Saloon, the girls had to either sing or dance at least once a night. Usually in their blue jeans or whatever they wore to work. They'd been working on the Cowboy Masquerade Ball routine before the bar opened for the past two weeks. But she hadn't been there when they'd discussed the costume. "You want me to dress as a whore?"

"No, sweetie. As a saloon girl. We *are* a saloon." She shoved the outfit into Libby's arms and spun her toward the bathroom. "Now, hurry before I start crying again."

Libby dashed out of the storeroom before she broke down in a big fit of boohoos, something she hadn't done since she'd left New York and swore she never would again. What was the saying? Oh, yeah.

*Never say never.*

MARK STOOD in front of the mirror, his crisp white shirt tucked into black jeans, the large silver buckle he'd won at the Houston rodeo for bronco riding gleamed from the good polishing he'd given it. He slid the black mask over his eyes and crammed the white cowboy hat on his head. "How do I look?"

Luke stepped up beside him, adjusting the bolero tie he'd chosen for the Cowboy Masquerade Ball at the Ugly Stick Saloon. "Like a redneck Lone Ranger."

He clapped Mark on the back. "She'll think you're hot stuff."

"What's with the Mexican caballero outfit?" Mark asked.

"I was going for the Zorro look. Is it too much?" He tied the black mask in place and settled the black hat on his head.

"No, you look dangerous. Girls like that." Mark frowned in the mirror. "Maybe I should change into something darker."

"No, don't. Women also like a white knight to rescue them. You've got that written all over you."

"Maybe we should swap. You usually have the rescue role."

"Not always." Luke rested a hand on his brother's shoulder. "I think it's fitting for the masquerade that you wear it, especially since I haven't managed any rescuing where Libby's concerned."

"Me either." Mark sat on the edge of his bed and pulled on his cowboy boots. "Something about her tells me she needs rescuing."

"Yeah. I felt it too." Luke held out his hands. "That's why I chose Zorro. He might wear black, but he's always bailing someone out. And I didn't want us to go dressed alike. I think Libby likes that we're so much alike, but that we're also different."

Mark sighed and shoved his hands in his pocket. "I could spend the rest of my life trying to please that woman."

"Me too." Luke sucked in a deep breath and let it out slowly. "She's incredible."

"What do you make of her insisting on no commitment?" Mark asked.

"I'm taking it as a challenge." Luke stared across at his brother, his eyes intensely black. "She's perfect for us."

Mark nodded. "My feelings exactly."

"You think she'll actually leave like she told Audrey?"

"I don't know. After yesterday, I was pretty sure she wouldn't leave." Mark pulled his white cowboy hat from his head. "But we haven't seen her since this morning and now I'm not sure at all." He twisted his hat brim in his hand, staring at the braid.

"Then what are we waiting for? We have to convince her that we're worth committing to." Luke headed for the door. "I refuse to give up. As long as Libby is still there, we have a chance."

Mark followed. "I'm with you, brother."

Twenty minutes later they struggled to find a parking space at the Ugly Stick Saloon.

"This Cowboy Masquerade Ball on the opening night of the rodeo was a good idea for saloon business, but I'm beginning to doubt we'll get two minutes alone with Libby." Mark dropped down from the pickup and waited for Luke.

"We'll either have to *make* the time to be with her or stay until they close. We need to talk to her."

"I'm for making time." Mark tugged at the black bandana he wore around his neck. "Come on, Zorro, let's do this."

Luke grinned. "If the Lone Ranger doesn't cut it with the lady, we're sunk."

As they stepped into the Ugly Stick Saloon, Mark laughed at all the Lone Rangers and Zorros already there.

Luke groaned. "How is Libby supposed to spot us in the crowd?"

"We'll make sure she does."

A few men had dressed as John Wayne, there were a couple Roy Rogers, a Wild Bill Hickok and a Doc Holiday. Many of the cowboys weren't wearing a mask, but a lot were.

The women wore a variety of costumes from Annie Oakley and Bell Starr to saloon girls in brightly colored corsets with flashy flounced skirts. All wore masks and smiled and flirted playfully with the men.

The band played a lively two-step and the floor was already crowded with dancers.

Mark made his way toward the bar where he hoped to find Libby popping open bottles of beer, filling mugs and flipping whiskey bottles to the delight of those near enough to see. A crowd of men gathered around the bar, all laughing and pushing each other to get closer.

As Mark neared, he glanced over the tops of their heads and stopped. His heart completed a full somer-sault and his breath caught in his throat. "Are you seein' what I'm seein'?"

Luke stood next to Mark, also craning to see, his eyes wide, a smile curling his lips into a huge, stupid grin. "Sweet Jesus, will you get a load of that costume?"

Mark shook his head, fully understanding why the men at the bar were fighting to get close. "And I didn't think Libby could get any hotter than the past twenty-four hours naked."

"Wow." Luke laid a hand on his chest. "Un-fuck-ing-believable."

Libby wore a mask over her beautiful green eyes, which didn't begin to disguise her long, curly auburn hair. But it was the sinful red corset cut so low that her breasts pushed up and spilled over the top like big, beautiful mushrooms, lending to a deep, dark cleavage that had every horny cowboy clamoring to crawl over the counter and claim her as his. Her skirt was a frilly, black thing with red ruffles and cut so short in front they could see the black matching panties. On her legs she wore black, net stockings ending in dangerously tall black stilettos. She tugged at the front of her corset, a frown denting her brows.

Mark's cock strained against his black jeans. "We won't get near her until someone leaves the bar," he shouted into Luke's ear.

"I don't think any of those men plan on leaving anytime soon." Luke touched Mark's sleeve and pointed to the right of the bar. "Come on. I see a table. We'll wait until she takes a break."

Mark didn't want to wait. Since he and Luke had kissed Libby goodbye that morning in front of the barn, he had been counting the minutes until he could be with her again.

Luke had been no better, stalking through the family home they shared with Jackson, unable to sit still for more than a minute at a time.

Kicking the chair from beneath the table, Mark straddled it and sat, facing the bar and Libby. She hadn't figured out who they were in their costumes, either that or she had, and was avoiding eye contact. No matter, the waiting was killing Mark and he'd just started.

Kendall Mason stopped in front of their table, carrying a tray of empty mugs and bottles and smiled.

Mark gave Kendall a cursory glance, noting that the costume was the same as the one Libby wore. But Kendall didn't look anything like Libby, nor did she inspire the same reaction. She leaned forward and tipped their hats up, giving them a generous view of the tops of her boobs. "Oh, hey, Mark, Luke. I thought it was you two. What can I get you boys?"

"Libby." Both Mark and Luke spoke at once.

Kendall laughed. "Sorry, not on the menu. You'll have to take it up with her when she gets off work."

Mark's lips twisted. He didn't want to wait. "Draft beer and a whiskey shooter."

"I'll have the same," Luke added.

"Got it." Kendall smiled. "I'll tell Libby you two are here."

Mark's gaze followed Kendall all the way back to the bar where she leaned over Libby's shoulder and spoke in her ear.

Libby's gaze shot up and over the crowd of men seated in front of her, panning the saloon until she saw them. For a moment her eyes lit and a smile curved her pretty lips.

Mark's cock jumped to attention beneath his fly. How she did that with just a smile made him shake his head. What was he, a randy teen with his first crush? Or was it that incredibly hot costume?

Then her eyes clouded and the smile faded. Libby turned away and reached for a bottle on the shelf behind her.

Luke leaned close "Did you see that?"

"Yeah." Mark frowned. "For a moment she looked happy to see us."

"Then she didn't." Luke sat back in his chair, his eyes narrowing behind his black Zorro mask. "Why?"

"I don't know, but I aim to figure it out tonight."

"Me too." Luke sat up straight, his head turning right then left. "Where's Audrey?"

The owner of the bar had her hair up on top of her head and wore an old-fashioned saloon-girl dress with a black corset and red skirt the exact opposite color combination from what Libby and the other waitresses wore. Audrey's dress was hiked up on one side, exposing a long length of her sexy legs. She wore a mask, but it did little to hide the fact she was the strawberry blonde beauty who'd purchased the Ugly Stick a couple years ago and brought it back to life.

"Over there. Looks like she's headed for the storeroom." Mark jumped to his feet, the movement sending his chair toppling over behind him. He set it straight and made a beeline for Audrey and the storeroom, though beeline might have been a stretch, considering the place was standing room only and everyone that could get in his way did.

By the time Mark and Luke reached the door to the storeroom, Audrey had disappeared inside.

Not one to be deterred, Mark had his hand on the doorknob and was turning it when a deep feminine growl erupted behind him.

"Where do you think you're going?"

He jumped, his hand leaving the knob as he turned to face Greta Sue. Wearing a fringed leather jacket, a leather hat and leather pants, she stood as tall as Mark and Luke and probably outweighed them by a good thirty pounds.

Luke stepped forward. "Hey, Greta Sue. You're looking fine tonight. Calamity Jane, isn't it?"

She nodded, her eyes narrowing. "That's right."

Luke smiled his best get-her-in-the-bed smile. "We'd like to talk with Audrey."

Greta crossed her arms over her chest and stood with her feet spread wide. "She's busy and you two know that the storeroom is off-limits to everyone but the staff."

"We'll only take a minute," Mark insisted, reaching for the knob.

Greta growled again, low and mean.

"Okay, okay." Mark backed up a step, raising his hands in surrender. If they had to wait for Audrey to come out, what was a few more minutes?

That few minutes felt like an hour, when in fact it was only about five before Audrey flung the door open and stepped out, her face flushed, mask askew and her skirt tucked into the back of the waistband of her net stockings.

When she spied Mark and Luke, her cheeks flamed. "Mark, Luke, what are you doing here?"

Before Mark could reply, a masked man in a John Wayne hat, vest and empty holster swaggered out behind Audrey.

"Holy hell, Jackson, you mean to tell me we've been waiting out here while you two catch a quickie in a closet?" Mark shook his head, laughing.

His oldest brother chuckled and tipped his hat, like the Duke. "Well, partner, I reckon we can't get privacy anywhere, can we now?"

Luke burst out laughing. "You two are too much."

Jackson's arm circled Audrey's waist. "Were you looking for me?"

"No, actually, we were looking for Audrey," Luke said.

Jackson shot a glance from Audrey to Mark and Luke, his forehead wrinkling beneath his mask. "What did I miss?"

Audrey's lips twisted as she fought to contain a grin that ultimately escaped. "What? You two don't tell your big brother everything?"

Audrey elbowed him in the gut. "They did Libby for the past twenty-four hours. You need to keep better tabs on your brothers."

"I thought you were working on your place." Jackson rubbed his ribs, his smile stretching across his face. "You did Libby, huh? I didn't think she liked men. I mean, I never saw her go out with anyone around these parts."

"Well, she went out with us," Mark said.

"The both of you?" Jackson's grin broadened. "Well, I'll be darned. And?"

"And nothing." Mark frowned. "We need to talk to her, Audrey. The sooner the better."

Audrey's smile faded. "Boys, I don't know what happened out there, but Libby is firm. This is her last night at the Ugly Stick Saloon and probably her last night in Temptation."

Mark's heart slipped into his gut like a ton of rocks. "She hasn't changed her mind?"

Audrey's lips straightened into a thin line. "She's quitting."

Luke shook his head, his dark face pale beneath the mask. "Why?"

"She didn't give me much of a reason, just said that she'd stayed too long and had to get away."

Mark backed against the wall and tried to breathe past the constriction in his throat. "She can't."

"I got her to promise to stay until after the masquerade ball. I don't want her to go. She's the best bartender I've ever had and besides that, she's been a good friend. A girl doesn't come by those too often."

"You have to make her change her mind." Luke stepped forward. "We need more time with her."

Audrey slipped an arm around Jackson's waist. "You think I haven't tried? She's pretty determined. If I could make her change her mind, I'd have done it by now. I was hoping you two could convince her."

Mark stared across at Luke. "How?"

"Oh, come on, boys." Jackson gave them his best disappointed-big-brother look. "You got Audrey and me together. Surely between the two of you, you'll come up with a way."

Luke hung his head, looking as much like a kicked puppy as a grown man could. "We can't make her stay if she doesn't want to."

Mark realized the truth of his twin's statement. Everything about Libby had pointed to her love of freedom—from her biker-babe, free-riding ways to the joy she'd shown at the open, light and airy feel of their home site. Making love on the deck, in the pool, on a horse, under the stars, had all been done in the open where the wind or sun caressed her naked beautiful skin. "We have to convince her."

"She's been adamant about no commitment," Luke reminded him.

Mark's fists clenched. "I thought she was giving herself an out."

"She did, and now she's taking it." Luke sighed.

"Do I detect the stench of defeat?" Jackson stood straight, his shoulders back, his head held high and proud like a Kiowa warrior. "My brothers, you shame me with your lack of courage. If you want the woman, go after her. Win her with your bravery, your chivalry and…"

Audrey laid a hand on Jackson's arm. "Win her with your heart. Libby doesn't like to be hemmed in. I think she's running from something. She wouldn't tell me what, but whatever it is keeps her on the move.

Find out what her dragon is, slay it and you just might convince her to stay."

Luke nodded. "Yes and no. We need to find out what makes her think she has to leave and clear that up, but we can't convince her to stay, we have to convince her that she can go anytime she likes."

"What?" Mark stared at his brother as if he had lost his mind.

"She needs to know that staying with us isn't caging her, it's her choice and she's free to leave anytime. We won't hold her back."

Audrey smiled. "Luke, I think you have it right. I'll see what I can do to get you three alone, but no guarantees. It's a madhouse tonight, and it doesn't look like it will slack up anytime soon."

"Thanks, Audrey." Mark touched her arm. "We'll do our best to make Libby happy."

"That's all that matters." Audrey hugged Jackson around the middle. "I'm glad I have you, dear."

"And me, you." Jackson dropped a kiss on her head. "Finding you and wooing you was way too much drama. I wouldn't want to go through that again."

When her brows rose into the hair hanging over her forehead, Jackson held up his hands. "But I would, if I had to. You're worth it." He pulled her into his arms and kissed her soundly.

Mark and Luke left the couple in a deep lip-lock and hurried back into the saloon's main room.

The band had taken a break and someone had put a bump-and-grind song on the stereo system.

A loud whoop went up from the entire room full of people as all eyes turned toward the bar.

Kendall, Lacey and Bella were being lifted up to the polished surface, where they joined Libby. The red corsets and skirts had every man in the place whistling and catcalling so loud, the music faded into the background.

When they lifted Charli up onto bar, she carried a microphone and leaned against one of the brace posts, one leg sliding up the other as she sang a dirty, sexy song while Kendall, Lacey, Bella and Libby danced in unison.

The crowd clapped in time, swaying to the sound, laughing and shouting, reaching out to touch the girls on the bar. One drunk cowboy made a grab for Libby's ankle and almost pulled it out from under her.

Mark lunged forward, ready to slam a fist into every one of the men who tried to grope Libby.

Luke's backhand across his chest stopped him before he'd gone two steps. "You can't. It's part of her job with the saloon."

"But I want to rip that guy a new asshole," Mark said through clenched teeth.

Libby pressed her stiletto to the man's forehead and pushed him back hard enough the crowd had to catch him.

Luke laughed. "The woman can hold her own."

The other men around him shoved the drunk to the rear, refusing to let him back up to the bar.

"Come on, we need to get to the front of that crowd. I want to talk to Libby." Mark nudged and pushed through the wall of men, all hollering for the dancers as they strutted, turned and ground their hips to the song Charli sang.

Luke followed right behind Mark as they made slow progress through the throng.

One man raised his fists, his face blotchy with anger and alcohol. "Hey, don't push me."

"Not trying to start a fight." Mark backed off, unwilling to get into brawl, when all he wanted was to get to Libby.

Luke slammed into Mark, and Mark bumped the man with the raised fists, shoving him against another guy.

Fist Man swung at Mark's face.

Mark shouted, "Duck!" He leaned right.

The fist whiffed past his ear and hit Luke in the jaw.

Luke staggered backward, stepping on the cowboy behind him and knocking him across a table.

Mark faced off with Fist Man and landed a punch in his breadbasket.

The man didn't even flinch, but his face reddened to a mottled patchwork and he let out a roar. He ducked his head and rammed into Mark's gut, rail-roading him through the crowd until he hit a table, slid across it and landed on his back on the floor, stunned and with the wind knocked out of his lungs.

Others who'd been flung or pushed aside leaped into the fray and fists flew unchecked.

Greta Sue muscled her way toward Mark, lifting him up off the floor. "You all right?"

Mark nodded, just beginning to breathe again. When he stood, he swayed, scanning the melee for his twin.

Luke faced off with Fist Man and another guy, holding his own in a two-to-one fist fight.

"I gotta make a call." Greta Sue let go of Mark and hurried toward the back of the bar and the telephone.

Charli had stopped singing, joining the girls on the bar in the fight to keep the groping hands from toppling them into the crowd.

Everyone was shouting and no one could hear anything, even the sound of sirens. Until the sheriff and five of his deputies pushed through the door. One raised a megaphone to his lips and announced, "Party's over."

Behind the deputies, one of the news reporters who'd come for the rodeo had his camera up, floodlights on, blinding the drunks and sober patrons alike.

Fist Man laid in one last punch, sending Luke flying backward into a chair that immediately tipped over backward.

Mark lunged for the cowboy, but never made it there.

A deputy grabbed him from behind and twisted his arm up behind him.

The noise died down and a voice could be heard booming over the others. "Give me that."

The megaphone gave a shrill whine and a voice blasted through the room. "Elizabeth Stratton, get down off that bar, immediately."

All eyes turned toward the sound. Mark glanced over his shoulder to see what they were staring at.

A man in a business suit fiddled with the megaphone and it blasted the room with another shrill squeal. He was flanked by two hulks also dressed in business suits looking more like giant apes playing dress-up. The man with the megaphone pointed at the bar and repeated, "Elizabeth Stratton, get down off that bar."

Luke picked himself off the floor and stood beside Mark. "Which one is Elizabeth Stratton?"

The deputy jerked Mark toward the door. "Come on, Lone Ranger, it's a night in the pokey for you."

"Wait." Mark jerked free of the deputy. He gazed toward the bar as Libby's face turned as white as a sheet and she fell forward into the crowd. "Libby!" Mark lunged forward, only to be stopped by a hand twisting his arm up between his shoulder blades. "Let me go. She could be hurt."

"The others caught her. There's a medic outside." The deputy grunted, holding tight to Mark. "You have more worries."

"I haven't done anything wrong," Mark insisted.

"I'd say disturbing the peace and disorderly conduct classify as wrongdoing. Now are you coming with me or do we add resisting arrest?"

Mark glanced at the man holding him. "Cramer, now is not the time to pay me back for stealing your date at prom six years ago."

Deputy Cramer smiled. "I'd say payback is long overdue. Keep moving."

Mark shouted over his shoulder. "Luke. Take care of Libby."

"I'll do what I can." Luke was already muscling his way through the crowd to where Libby had landed.

Mark glanced back as the deputy pushed him through the door and out into the clear Texas night sky.

Lights swirled on top of no less than five law enforcement vehicles and two ambulances that had come from both Temptation and Hole in the Wall to converge on the county line at the Ugly Stick Saloon.

As Deputy Cramer crammed him into the backseat of his SUV next to a passed-out drunk, reeking of puke and alcohol, Mark ground his teeth.

What had just happened in there? Why had Libby fainted? And what did it have to do with that man who'd called out for Elizabeth Stratton?

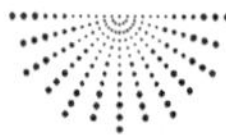

# CHAPTER NINE

*L*ibby perched on the side of a bed in the Emergency Room of the small hospital in Temptation, wishing there was a drug that would make her disappear. The white walls and sterile environment seemed to close in around her and she couldn't get out. She was waiting for the doctor to release her after her dramatic faint on the bar at the saloon.

"Where's my daughter?" a deep male voice echoed in the corridor.

"I'm sorry, sir. Who is your daughter?" a nurse's voice asked, patiently.

"Elizabeth Stratton."

Libby cringed and pulled the sheet up around her face, wishing she could hide.

A pause and then the nurse stated, "We don't have an Elizabeth Stratton listed. Perhaps she was taken to Amarillo?"

"She was brought here, I tell you," the man said.

"Perhaps you could describe her."

"Five feet six, red hair, green eyes. Twenty-five years old."

"The only woman we have by that description was brought here tonight from the Ugly Stick Saloon fight."

"Which room?" the man demanded.

Libby cringed, gathering the sheet and pushing it aside.

"I'm sorry, sir, unless you have proof you're family, visiting hours start at nine in the morning. You'll have to come back then."

"The hell I will." Footsteps pounded on the tiles and doors slammed against the walls as they were flung open one at a time down the hallway. "Elizabeth!"

Libby held her breath and waited for the door to fly open and all hell to break loose. If she'd thought it was bad in the saloon, it would be nothing compared to what was about to go down when her father finally caught up to her.

She slid out of the bed and raced for the window, but it was one of those kinds that never opened. Her gaze darted to the bathroom door, but before she could get there, her door slammed open and her father stood there, his towering frame filling the void, trapping her in the room.

Her heart fluttered in her chest and butterflies filled her belly as her life came full circle to when she was a prisoner in her own home, surrounded by wealth, duty and bodyguards. She sighed. "Hello, Daddy."

For a long moment, John Stratton stood there, his gaze raking over her.

Part of Libby rejoiced at seeing her father for the first time in two years. The other knew what it meant and rebelled at the loss of freedom.

"Where the hell have you been for the past two years, girl?" he demanded, his face flushing a deep, ruddy red.

She ignored his question and glanced beyond him, her brows rising. "Where are your bodyguards, Daddy? You never go anywhere without them."

"They're on their way to the jail in some town called Hole In The Wall, damn it." He poked a finger toward her. "No thanks to you. That'll be our next stop once I get you out of this place."

Libby's fists tightened. Standing barefoot in her hospital gown, she knew she didn't look like a force to be reckoned with, but she hadn't lived two years on her own without growing a backbone.

"Sir, you really cannot disturb the patients at this hour." A nurse stood behind her father, holding a clipboard chart in both hands, evidently ready to use it if the man got violent. "I've called the police. If you don't leave, they'll arrest you for disturbing the peace."

"I don't give a rat's ass what the police do. This is my goddamn daughter and she's coming with me, now."

Libby's chin tipped up. "No, Daddy, I'm not."

"You damn well better."

"Or what?" She shook her head. "You'll cut me off?"

He frowned.

"In case you hadn't noticed, I haven't asked for a cent from you in the past two years. Not one." She stepped forward, her chest pushing out. "I've been free of you, your money and bodyguards all that time and nothing bad has happened to me."

His eyes narrowed. "Now that the media knows you're here, you'll be in danger."

"I don't care. I wish you would disinherit me so that none of them will care if I'm alive or dead."

"Damn it, Elizabeth, be reasonable."

"No, you be reasonable." She crossed her arms over her chest. "I'm not going back to New York. I like it here." As she said the words, her heart flooded with a familiar warmth that she'd found only here in Temptation, Texas. A warmth that had more to do with the people than the weather.

"You've played long enough. You need to come home and be a part of this family." He grabbed her arm and dragged her toward the door.

"What family? Ever since Mamma died, it's been you ruling the world. I never had a say in my life. Well, now I do." She dug her bare heels into the cool tile and leaned away from the arm holding her. "I'm not going."

A sheriff's deputy stepped up behind her father, his hand resting on the nine-millimeter pistol in his holster. "Sir, release the woman and step out into the hallway." The lawman reached for John Stratton's arm.

"She's not a woman, she's just a girl, dammit." Libby's father jerked his arm away from the deputy. "I resent being treated like a criminal."

"Then let go of the woman, and leave the building immediately." The deputy stared down his nose at John Stratton, his hand resting on his pistol grip. "Or I'll be forced to arrest you for disturbing the peace and assault."

"Daddy, let go," Libby said in a calm, clear tone.

"Tell them that you're my daughter and that you're coming with me," her father demanded.

"I am your daughter." She gave a half smile, her chest squeezing at what she had to do. "But I'm not going with you."

Her father's face darkened. "It's that saloon you were working at, isn't it?"

She snorted softly. "No, it's not the Ugly Stick."

"Then it's some man."

Her heart fluttered as an image of Mark and Luke rising naked out of the pool filled her mind. Some of her feelings must have shown on her face.

Her father's eyes narrowed. "I knew it. I'll have him arrested for—"

"For what, Daddy?" Libby planted her fists on her hips. Standing in her hospital gown, she knew she was no match for her father, but she refused to back down ever again. "For caring about me? For taking the time to get to know me and what I like? For allowing me the freedom to choose?"

"Well, no. For brainwashing you into thinking that living in a backwater town with a bunch of hicks is better than taking your position in society as the daughter of—"

"The multi-billionaire John Stratton?" She shook her head. "I want nothing to do with that life. I left it behind and won't go back."

"You have to," her father argued.

"In case you haven't noticed, I'm twenty-five years old and can legally make my own decisions. I don't have to go with you."

"Sir, for the last time, I'm asking you to leave peacefully." The deputy's hands hovered over his utility belt.

"Go, Daddy," Libby urged her father. "Before you get in trouble."

He planted his fists on his hips and braced his feet wide on the tiles. "I'm not leaving without you."

In a flash of movement, the deputy snapped a handcuff onto John Stratton's wrist and jerked his arm up between his shoulder blades, pushing him against the wall. "Sir, I warned you, now you'll have to take a ride with me down to the jailhouse."

"This is an outrage!" Libby's father shouted, his voice ringing out against the sterile walls of the small hospital.

The few patients that could stand leaned in the doorways of their rooms, peering out at the ruckus going on in the corridor.

Libby shook her head, righteous indignation

fading into sadness as the deputy hauled her father away.

"I'll have your job for this," her father shouted at the officer as he was manhandled through the hallway and out of the hospital.

Libby couldn't wait for the doctor to release her, she had to leave now, before her father was freed on bond and before he had the chance to bail out his bodyguards and assign one of them to tail her.

She grabbed the only clothing she had, the floozy skirt and corset and the stilettos, slipped into them quickly and marched herself past the nurse's desk.

"Where are you going, Miss Jones?" The nurse at the station leaned over the counter. "You need to wait for the doctor to release you."

"I can't. I have to get out of here." Libby left the hospital behind and made her way to a twenty-four-hour convenience store where she asked to borrow the telephone.

Audrey answered on the first ring. "Ugly Stick Saloon. We're closed."

"Audrey, I need you to pick me up from the Gas 'N Sip down the street from the hospital."

"Libby? Are you all right?"

"I'm fine, I just need a ride back to my bike."

"I'll be there in fifteen minutes."

Libby hung up, chest aching, and found a quiet corner of the store to hide in and plan her escape from her father, her former life and the new life and place she'd come to love so much.

SHERIFF THOMAS GUIDED Luke to the big jail cell where Mark and several other men sat on benches attached to the wall.

As he unlocked the jail cell, the sheriff waved Luke inside. "I wouldn't have arrested you if I hadn't witnessed you hitting Reggie Finkle. Finkle has you up on charges of assault."

"Did you ask him who threw the first punch? At least get the story straight before you lock me up." Luke balked at stepping through. "I really need to get to the hospital and check on a friend. Please don't do this."

"I'm sorry, Luke. The county judge came in special for this mess and set bail on you boys. Until someone comes to post your bail, you're in for the night."

Luke entered the cell and the bars swung closed behind him with a final metal clank. He turned and clung to the rails. "Please, Sheriff, I have to get to the hospital. If I don't, she might be gone when I get out of here."

The sheriff shook his head. "Should have thought of that before you took that swing."

A deputy leading a man down the corridor toward the cell where Mark and Luke leaned against the bars pulled his charge to the side to allow the sheriff to pass.

The man was dressed in a wrinkled business suit, shirt untucked, tie askew, his gray hair standing on end, like he'd been in a tussle. "Let me go, or you will regret it."

"I've never had more pleasure than I'm having

right now." The deputy unlocked the cell and shoved the man inside, twisting the key in the lock with a decided flourish. "You need time to cool off, mister."

"I'll have your job for this, damn it! You can't treat John Stratton this way." The man shook a fist through the bar.

Mark laid a hand on Luke's shoulder. "Come on, Luke. The sheriff and his deputies aren't putting up with much tonight. I hear Nelson Bailey is at the emergency room now with a broken nose and two other deputies have fractured ribs."

"But she'll leave and we won't know where to find her." Luke gripped the bars in his fists, testing their strength, wishing he could bend them and escape.

"If she leaves, it's her choice," Mark said. "We can't hold her. Haven't you been saying that all along?"

Luke hung his head. "Yeah. But we needed more time with her."

"Goddamit, if my daughter leaves town before I get out of here, I'll sue this city for everything it's worth, do you hear me?" The businessman grabbed the bars and tried to shake them.

None of the sheriff's deputies listened.

"Two years," the man shouted to the air. "It's taken me two years to find her, and I finally catch up to her in this godforsaken town."

"They're not listening." Mark glanced at the man who'd arrived last.

"Two years?" Luke recalled something Libby had said their first night together about two years.

"Hey, aren't you the man who was shouting at the

Ugly Stick Saloon for someone to get off the bar?" Mark asked.

The man kicked the bars and winced, reaching for his foot and the patent leather shoe he'd scuffed in the process. "What's it to you?"

"We were there. Who were you yelling at?" Luke shoved his hand through his hair, trying to get his mind off Libby and failing miserably.

"My daughter, Elizabeth. She was dancing on the bar dressed as a goddamn whore."

Mark sighed and dropped onto a bench, burying his face in his hands. "It was Cowboy Masquerade night at the Ugly Stick Saloon. Audrey has her staff dress the part of saloon girls."

"Elizabeth?" Luke shook his head, a chill slithering across his skin. "None of the girls who work at the saloon go by that name. Perhaps you were mistaken."

The businessman frowned and paced the length of the cell, stepping over the legs of a man passed out on the floor. "I know my daughter. She was up there, acting like a tramp. You'd think she would have a little more pride than to do what she was doing."

"What was wrong with what they were doing?" Luke asked. "The girls hire on because they can dance or sing. It's part of the requirement. Not everyone makes the cut. And the pay's good."

"I didn't pay good money on classical ballet lessons for my daughter to dance burlesque in a saloon."

"Maybe she didn't want to dance ballet." Mark stared up at the man. "Maybe she likes burlesque. Did you ever consider what she likes?"

"A Stratton does not exhibit disgusting behavior in public. It's okay behind closed bedroom doors, but not where the paparazzi can get hold of it and plaster it all over the newspapers. It'll ruin her reputation."

Luke stared at the man. Something about his green eyes and the stubborn way he lifted his chin looked strangely familiar.

No. Luke shook his head. He was seeing things that weren't there. Wasn't he? "Sounds like you're more worried about what others think than whether or not your daughter is happy."

"What do you know?" The man's sneer told Luke exactly what this man's opinion was of him. "You're nothing but a beer-drinking, skirt-chasing cowboy. Look where you are—in a jail cell with a bunch of drunken misfits."

Mark laughed out loud. "Careful pointing fingers, mister. You're in the same jail cell."

The man opened his mouth, his face reddening. He must have thought better of saying anything because he closed his mouth and sat on the other end of the bench Mark was seated on. "I don't know what to do to get through to her."

"We know the feeling," Mark commiserated.

"I haven't seen my daughter in two years, and she has me thrown in jail for trying to talk sense into her. I just want her to come home." He leaned his elbows on his knees and scrubbed his hands across his face, looking older than he had when he entered the cell.

Luke leaned his back against the bars. "Did you

ever think your daughter might not want the kind of life you lead?"

The man snorted. "It's for the best."

"The best for who?"

"How can I keep her safe, if I don't know where she is? She needs protection." Stratton looked up at Luke, his face gaunt, his eyes almost sunken.

"From what?" Luke held his hands out. "Even a gilded cage is still a cage."

The older man who'd come in blustering and demanding justice now sat with his head in his hands. "I can't lose her again. She's all I have left."

"You've been looking for two years?" Mark straightened, his eyes narrowing. "Sir, which one of the girls on the bar tonight is your daughter?"

"Elizabeth, the pretty one."

Damn, had his instincts had been right? Luke held his breath knowing what was coming next.

"The one with the red hair and green eyes." He smiled, a single tear trailing down his wrinkled cheek. "Looks just like her mother, God rest her soul. But she has my eyes."

"Holy hell." Mark stared across at Luke. "Libby."

The old man sighed. "The confounded woman at the hospital said her name was Libby Jones. Well, it's not. It's Elizabeth Stratton, of the Manhattan Strattons."

All the air left Luke's lungs as if someone had punched him in the breadbasket. "Libby is Elizabeth Stratton? The heiress who disappeared from New York City two years ago?"

The man nodded, glancing across at him. "Do you know her? My private investigators got a tip from a cop at my local Manhattan precinct that the deputy sheriff from this town was searching through New York City missing persons looking for a woman meeting my daughter's description. It's the first lead I've had worth following in a long time. I couldn't believe it. She must be really down on her luck to have ended up here."

"Why do you say that?" Luke stood tall. "Temptation is a much nicer place to live than in a high-rise in a huge city."

"How do you know?" John Stratton asked. "Have you ever lived in a high-rise? There is so much more to offer in a big city than in a hole in the wall like this."

"Hole In The Wall is on the other side of the county line and it's not such a bad place either." Mark stood, his chest swelling out. "Sir, you need to test the water before you declare it unfit to drink."

"Elizabeth has a fine education. She's wasting it in a saloon. She could be—should be—training to run Stratton Enterprises when I step down."

"Again, what if she doesn't want it?" Luke asked.

"Damn it, what she wants doesn't matter!" The older man stood, frowning fiercely, his fists clenched.

Luke faced him, standing toe-to-toe, his cowboy boots lining up with the man's expensive leather dress shoes. "You don't know your daughter at all, do you, Mr. Stratton?"

"I know she doesn't belong in this godforsaken town," he said, his nose inches from Luke's.

Mark stood beside Luke in a stare-down with the billionaire John Stratton, his face set in stone, a muscle twitching in his jaw. "I can see why she ran away from you, and I feel really sorry for her if you end up dragging her back to the city."

Stratton pulled himself up straight, his shoulders back. "It's where she belongs."

"We don't think so," Luke said.

"Are you the man she fancies herself in love with?" The old man's eyes narrowed as he faced Luke. "I'm warning you, don't get between me and my daughter."

"Or what?" Luke crossed his arms over his chest.

"Or I'll make your life miserable."

Luke shook his head. "I doubt you could make my life as miserable as you've made your own."

Stratton shook his head. "Wanna bet?"

Mark poked a finger in Stratton's chest. "From what we've learned about Libby—"

"Her name's Elizabeth, not Libby." Stratton's nose and lip twitched into a sneer.

Mark continued as if Stratton had never spoken, "Libby values her freedom so much, she'll keep moving rather than give it up."

"Are you willing to lose her again?" Luke asked.

"I have detectives and private investigators."

"They took two years to find her this time." Mark's brows rose. "Are you willing to wait another two years to see your daughter again?"

Stratton breathed out his nose like a bull in the ring, once, twice, then backed up and sighed. "No."

"And we don't want to lose her either." Luke laid a hand on Stratton's arm. "If you truly want your daughter to be a part of your life, you'll have to give her the freedom she has worked so hard to preserve."

"And you?" he asked. "Which one of you is in love with my daughter?"

"I am." Luke said at the same time as his brother.

John Stratton laughed and shook his head. "You both can't have her."

Mark grinned. "We think we can."

The older man coughed and sputtered. "Both? It's indecent, if you ask me."

"We love her," Luke said. "Which seems to be more than can be said for you."

"I love my daughter," John Stratton stated. "I want only what's best for her."

Luke squeezed the man's arm. "Then let her go."

"No." The older man shook his head. "I can't. And what makes you think you can hold her any more than I could?"

"We wouldn't try to hold her." Luke spread his hands out wide. "She would have to make a choice to stay. That will be completely up to her."

"Mark, Luke, you're sprung." Jackson and one of the deputies entered the corridor between the jail cells. "Come on, it's late, let's go home."

The deputy unlocked the cell and jerked his head. "The twins can go."

When Stratton made a move to leave the cell with them, the deputy stepped in front of him. "Not you."

Luke stuck out a hand to stop his older brother from leaving. "Jackson, you got enough money to bail this man out?"

Mark glared at his twin. "What are you doing?"

"He's Libby's father." Luke looked back at the older man, who seemed to be aging by the second.

Mark snorted. "And if he has his way, he'll take her back to New York. You know she'd hate it."

"I know." Luke tipped his head toward the older Stratton. "I also know that she won't stop running until her father stops chasing her."

Mark stared at his brother long and hard before he nodded. "Damn, I hate it when you're right." He turned to his older brother. "Jackson, can you spring the old man?"

Jackson's brows rose. "I don't know. How much will it take?"

"I don't want your damn charity," Stratton said. "My people will front the money."

"When you get a hold of them." Jackson crossed his arms over his chest. "From what the sheriff told me, your bodyguards are in the jail in Hole In The Wall, not much good they're doing you there."

The businessman straightened his collar, pushing his shoulders back. "My lawyer will take care of everything."

The deputy shook his head. "I called that number you gave us several times. All I got was an answering machine. You'll be waiting until morning."

Stratton's lips thinned and he stared through the bars at the Gray Wolf brothers.

Luke almost laughed at the disgusted look of desperation on Stratton's face.

The old man hated asking for help, but Luke had no doubt he would, if he wanted to see his daughter badly enough.

"Do you want our help or not?" Mark demanded.

"Yes," Stratton said grudgingly.

"Then say please." Luke spoke quietly, but his words held a hint of steel.

The old man sucked in a deep breath and let it out. "Please."

Jackson wrote a check to bail John Stratton out of jail.

Once outside, Stratton glanced around at Main Street in the small town of Temptation. "What now?"

"You're going to our house with Jackson. Mark and I are going after Libby."

"I can't stand by and risk losing her again," Stratton said. "I want to go with you."

Luke shook his head. "Not this time."

"But I need to talk to her."

"And if you can promise not to threaten her with taking her back to New York, we'll do our best to get her to talk to you." Luke's brows dipped. "Can you make that promise?"

Stratton frowned deeply and nodded. "I promise."

"I don't trust him," Mark said.

The older man pulled himself up to stand eye-to-eye with Mark, every bit as tall as the Gray Wolfs. "A Stratton's word is gold."

"And gold didn't buy your daughter's love, did it?" Luke nodded. "In the meantime, we need a ride to the Ugly Stick so we can get our truck."

Jackson dropped them off at the saloon and took off to the Gray Wolf Ranch with an unhappy John Stratton.

"Think he'll keep his promise?" Mark asked.

Luke grinned. "A Stratton's promise is gold. Come on, we have to find Libby before she makes a run for it." Luke jogged to the back of the building and was standing there, his heart fluttering inside his chest when Mark caught up. "Her bike's gone."

"That doesn't mean she's made it out of town yet." Mark grabbed Luke's arm and pulled him back around the front to their truck. "She'll want to pack a few things first."

Luke climbed into the truck and sat behind the steering wheel, his fingers on the keys in the ignition, his chest tight, a lump forming in his throat. "We can't let her leave without at least talking to her first."

"I'm on it." Mark pulled his cell phone and punched in some numbers. "Cramer, it's Mark Gray Wolf. I need you to put out an APB or whatever it takes on a woman driving a Harley Davidson headed out of town. I don't care which way she's heading, just stop her and call me ASAP. You owe me for throwing me in jail. Six years is a long time to hold a grudge. I'll tell your wife why you jailed me if you don't do this little favor for me." Mark paused. "Thought so.

Thanks, pal." He clicked the off button. "That should keep her from making it out of town before we have a chance to talk to her."

Luke shifted into drive and spun out of the gravel parking lot. "Where do you think she's gone?"

Mark stared out the windshield, his gaze and focus on the road ahead. "Let's hit her apartment first."

AFTER AUDREY HAD DROPPED her off at her bike, Libby had swung by her apartment and shoved as much as she could in one bag. Leaving an envelope on the counter for her landlord with the next month's rent money, she left the apartment and pushed the key through the mail slot. A lump rose in her throat. This had been her home for eight months, the longest she'd stayed anywhere in her two-year stint in hiding. Well, it couldn't be helped. If she wanted to retain her freedom, moving on was the only answer.

To keep from being seen by any of her father's stalkers, Libby had parked at the rear of the old house that had been divided into four individual apartments. As she strapped her bag to the back of her motorcycle seat, she glanced around several times, fully expecting someone to jump out, grab her and drag her kicking and screaming back to New York.

"What am I doing?" She straightened, her hands falling to her sides, the realization that she didn't have to go with her father really sinking in for the first time. He didn't have that kind of hold on her anymore and hadn't since she'd turned eighteen. She was an adult now, and didn't have to run from her father's influence. Then why was she?

Libby stared at her apartment building, a ramshackle old house built in the fifties, and she almost cried. Why did she have to leave? She was twenty-five, fully capable of making her own decisions, of living her own life and finding her own way. She'd changed her name to avoid the paparazzi, and so far that had been enough to keep her well below the radar of the media. But not her father's investigators.

So what? Maybe it was time to push back, time to stop running and stand up to her father and the media nightmare that was part of being a Stratton. She'd taken the first step in the hospital by telling her father that she wasn't going with him. Hell, she'd had him hauled off to jail.

A twinge of guilt twisted around her heart. Knowing her father's lawyers, he'd be out before the night was over. The news reporters would get wind and make a big story about nothing, and Libby's cover would probably be blown, but it didn't matter.

She liked it here in Temptation, working at the Ugly Stick Saloon, seeing the Gray Wolf brothers.

Libby sighed, wishing they were there now. When she was with Mark and Luke, they gave her all the affection she craved, without crowding her, letting her know that she could call the shots, that she could leave whenever she liked. They didn't want to be with her because she was the daughter of a very wealthy man. They wanted to be with her because they liked her for who she was. She smiled. They'd wanted to take her out since the day she'd started work at the saloon. How stupid to have put them off for so long.

Damn it, she wanted to stay and see where things would go with the twins. A flutter of excitement hit her full in the gut, spreading warmth lower to the junction of her thighs. She'd never be bored with Mark and Luke, never feel the wanderlust so many of the men she'd met had inspired.

"I'm not leaving." She spoke into the night sky, as if by saying the words out loud, she couldn't take them back.

Standing beside her bike, she stared up at the old house and swore. Since she'd pushed her key back into her apartment, she was locked out and refused to call the landlord in the middle of the night to let her in.

She still had the key to the Ugly Stick Saloon she'd meant to drop off on her way out of town. If she wanted, she could camp out there for the night and contact her landlord in the morning. Her head tipped back, and she stared up at the stars, washed out by the streetlights. Suddenly it seemed very important that she see the stars, free of the lights from town. Stars she'd never seen from the streets of New York City, the city that never slept. A city plagued with light pollution to the point that the night sky was only the dark abyss beyond the neon signs and glare.

Libby swung her leg over the bike seat and pulled away from Temptation, choosing a back road out of town, not the main roads lined with streetlights. The sooner she could see the stars, the better.

Soon pavement led to gravel and she found herself on the unimproved road leading out to the only place she'd been truly happy in the past two years. A place where she could think, and where she'd see so many stars she could count them until she grew old.

MARK TOOK the steps up to Libby's apartment two at a time and banged on the door. "Libby!" He listened and waited. Nothing.

Luke arrived at the top of the stairs and pounded again. "Libby!"

The old man who lived below her apartment poked his head out of his front door. "Hey, keep it down up there. Some of us are trying to sleep." The old man started to close the door, grumbling. "All the coming and going, motorcycle engines, it's a surprise if anyone gets any shuteye."

"Motorcycle engines?" Luke vaulted to the bottom of the steps and stuck his foot in the door before the old man could fully close it. "Did you say motorcycle engines?"

"Yeah. That young lady from upstairs revved her engine about ten minutes ago and blasted me out of a darned good dream."

"Ten minutes?" Luke grabbed the man's arms. "Are you sure?"

The old guy brushed Luke's hands away. "Of course I'm sure. I looked at my clock when she did it."

Mark met Luke at the bottom of the steps, pulling his cell phone from his pocket, dread filling his heart. "I'm calling."

Deputy Cramer answered on the third ring. "No one's seen the woman on the bike. You are talking about Libby Jones, aren't you?"

"Yes, we're looking for Libby."

"You do know her name isn't Libby, don't you?"

"It's Elizabeth Stratton, we know. Are you sure the others were looking?"

"There's only one main road in and out of town. Both directions were covered. Sorry, dude."

"Thanks anyway." Mark clicked the off button and shoved the phone into his pocket, his heart hitting the bottom of his belly. "We lost her."

"How could she have gotten by without them seeing her?" Luke shook his head. "She had to have gone out the highway."

A spark of hope ignited in Mark's chest. "Unless she didn't leave."

"She's not at her apartment. We've been to the Ugly Stick. Where else would she have gone?"

Mark backhanded his brother in the chest. "Where do we go when we want to think?" He took off running for the pickup, where he jumped in behind the steering wheel.

"Skyview? You think she's gone there?" Luke loped after Mark, sliding into the passenger seat, tossing the keys to his brother. "I hope you're right."

"Think about it." Mark switched on the engine and jammed the shift into reverse. "She said it was the only place she'd found in two years where she felt completely free."

"But her father's in town. He's who she was running from in the first place." Luke stared ahead into the darkness. "You'd think she'd keep running."

Mark grinned. "Unless she's tired of running."

"And she wants to put down roots." Luke's face broke into a smile.

"With the two men who showed her what free-riding was all about." Mark prayed he was right.

Luke raised a hand. "Don't get ahead of yourself, brother. She has the power to break our hearts."

"Or make us whole. I choose to believe she wants to stay." Mark turned down one of the streets leading to the edge of town that became a dirt road as soon as they cleared city limits. He didn't slow on the gravel, bumping along as fast as he could, determined to catch up to the woman they'd both grown to love. He had to be right. Or if she hadn't decided to stay, and if she had gone to Skyview, at least Mark hoped it meant she'd consider staying.

"What if she's not there?" Luke said into the dark cab.

"She will be." Mark pressed his foot to the accelerator, kicking up dust and gravel behind the pickup.

When they arrived at Skyview, they didn't see Libby or her bike.

Mark's chest tightened as he climbed down from the truck and ran toward the house.

"She's not here," Luke called out, racing to catch up.

"She has to be." Mark rounded the corner of the building to the other side where the moon shone down on the deck, lighting it like shadowed sunshine.

Stretched out on the wooden planks, her naked body gleaming a bluish-silver in the moonlight, lay Libby. She leaned up on one elbow and stared across the distance at Mark and Luke. "About time you two got here."

Mark laughed out loud and loped to the deck, dropping down beside her, his gaze panning her beautiful length. "How'd you know we'd come?"

"I didn't. But a girl can always hope the men she loves will read her mind."

Luke stopped with one foot on the steps leading up to the deck. "Love?" He took another step up. "That's a pretty powerful word you're using there, young lady."

She lay back and stared up at the stars. "I know."

Mark reached out and cupped her face in his palm. Though he ached to touch all the other parts of her body, he knew they had to get a few things straight first. "You didn't leave."

"Nope." She smiled. "I couldn't."

"Why?" Luke dropped down to the deck beside her.

"Because I had too many reasons not to." She raised her arms over her head, arching her back, her nipples tight little peaks on her perky breasts.

Mark longed to touch, to pull one of those pretty little buds into his mouth and suck hard, but he had to know she wasn't playing with them, leading them on only to leave when morning dawned.

"So you're staying?" Luke asked what was on Mark's mind.

Libby nodded. "Can't think of a place I've liked better."

Mark's fists clenched to keep him from skimming his fingers along the curves of her body. "For how long?"

She leaned up on her hands. "Good grief. You have a naked woman lying in front of you, the moon is shining and, short of candles, the setting is perfect. What does a girl have to do to get a couple of guys interested?"

Luke bunched his fists, but remained hands-off.

Mark knew it had to be killing his brother as much as it was killing him. He couldn't force words past his constricted throat.

"Mark and I care about you," Luke stated, the more eloquent of the two.

With a pout, Libby sat up all the way. "Apparently not enough to make love to me."

Mark shook his head. "That's where you're wrong. We care enough not to make love until we know where we stand and whether or not you'll be gone tomorrow."

"I'm here, aren't I?" She raised a hand, starlight glimmering off the tears pooling in her eyes. "I can't promise more."

"We can't take less." Luke reached out and

thumbed away a tear slipping down her cheek. "I love you too much to lose you now."

"And I love you too. The thought of losing you…" Mark's fingers slid down over her shoulder, capturing her hand. "We thought you'd left us tonight. It nearly broke my heart." He pressed her hand to his chest. "I want to know you'll be here longer than just one night."

"Me too." Luke leaned in and pressed a gentle kiss to her lips.

"Question is, do you really love us enough to stay?" Mark asked.

She laughed, the sound catching on a sob. "Am I enough woman for both of you to love? Will I be able to satisfy you?"

Joy burgeoned in Mark's heart. "Baby, you're amazing and you can do anything you set your mind to."

"I'm just now beginning to believe that about myself." She lifted Mark's hand and rubbed it against her cheek. "I've been running for so long, I didn't stop to think about what I was running from. It took finally getting caught to realize I was running from myself. I didn't want to stand up and fight for what I wanted." She snorted. "My father can be a very intimidating man."

Luke smiled. "We know."

Her eyes widened. "You know?"

Mark grinned. "We spent some time in jail with him."

Libby cringed. "He wouldn't let go of me in the

hospital, and then the deputy hauled him off. I felt so guilty."

"Don't worry." Mark's lips twisted. "Jackson bailed him out. Seems his attorney wasn't answering his calls and his bodyguards were incarcerated in Hole In The Wall's jail."

Libby chuckled. "That had to make him mad. He's used to having everyone at his beck and call."

"Yeah, I gathered that." Mark squeezed her hand. "He hated that we bailed him out, but he accepted the offer."

Luke pushed her hair back and dropped a kiss on her shoulder. "Your father is at the ranch house now with Jackson."

Libby sat up straighter. "You brought my father to the ranch?"

Mark nodded. "Yeah, seems he's had some revelations of his own and wants a chance to talk to you. We made him promise not to pressure you into going back to New York."

"He knows I won't go." Libby stared down at her hands. "I love it too much here. I love you two."

Mark winced. "Yeah, well he wasn't too thrilled with the idea of you being with both of us."

Libby's chin lifted. "If he wants to be a part of my life, he'll have to accept you two." She sighed and looked up at the two men. "I'm not ready to talk to him now—we can convince him tomorrow. I've got other things to occupy my thoughts and time here." She smiled, the moon shining in her eyes.

"Take all the time you need, darlin'." Luke cupped her face again. "We've got all night."

"And we'd love to show you how much we want you to stay." Mark's hand slipped across her knee and up to the juncture of her thighs, where her soft curls beckoned to him.

Luke moved closer on her other side. "We don't want you to feel trapped."

"But we want you around." Mark bent to capture one of her nipples between his teeth, nipping softly.

Luke laid her back on the deck, his hands roving over her other breast. "We love you."

LIBBY LAY back on the hard wood of the deck with nothing but the sky and Mark and Luke's hands covering her. "Enough talk, and too many clothes. If you truly love me, show me."

Mark and Luke leapt to their feet and shucked clothes so fast, Libby laughed out loud.

When they lay down beside her, she sighed, her legs falling open, her heart winging to the sky. She'd never felt so free and so loved as she did at that moment.

Mark slipped a finger into her, stroking the rush of juices out to her clit where he circled over and over, drawing a gasp from her lips.

Luke bent to claim a nipple, sucking it deep into his mouth, teasing the tip with his tongue, catching it between his teeth and nipping.

Libby cupped the back of Luke's head, loving that

he was the thinker and was so thoughtful, while Mark was the man to jump in and make things happen. The two complemented each other and she loved them both for who they were.

"Make love to me, my Gray Wolf men." She rolled to her side, facing Mark.

Luke rested his hand on her hips and nudged her entrance from behind with his cock.

Mark stroked her clit, lathering it with her own, musky juices, strumming her to a frenzy as Luke thrust inside, filling her to full, pumping deep.

She loved these two men who'd given her everything, including her freedom.

As she rocketed over the edge of orgasm, she cried out their names, thankful to whatever Indian gods they prayed to for bringing these men to her.

# BOOTS & BAREBACK

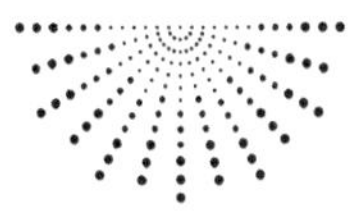

UGLY STICK SALOON BOOK #5

*New York Times & USA Today*
Bestselling Author

ELLE JAMES
*writing as*
MYLA JACKSON

BOOTS & BAREBACK
UGLY STICK SALOON
New York Times Bestselling Author
ELLE JAMES
writing as
MYLA JACKSON

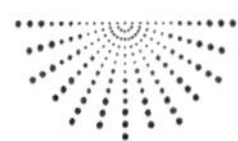

"**W**ell, I reckon it'll do for a bachelor party. Mind if your old man comes along for a beer?" Jonathon O'Brien, owner of the Rockin' O Ranch hadn't seen the inside of the Ugly Stick Saloon for a couple years. He hadn't felt much like getting out since his wife had died of breast cancer.

"What's not to love about this place?" Gabe, Jonathon's oldest son, waved a hand at the crowded interior of the Ugly Stick. "It's got atmosphere."

"They can provide the whiskey and stripper," Tanner, the second oldest, noted. "That's all we need."

"Don't be such an ass." Sean elbowed his older brother.

"Why's that being as ass?" Tanner frowned. "So I like women. The nakeder the better. And that makes me an ass? I don't see you turning down the fairer sex."

"Point made." Sean chuckled. "But you're still an ass."

Tanner punched his brother in the arm. "Yeah, but you're my brother. Takes one to know one."

"Can you quit jackin' around and focus?" Gabe interceded. "We're here to commission this place for our little brother's bachelor party."

Jonathon shook his head, staring around the table at three of his four sons, his only daughter around the joint somewhere, waiting tables. "I can't get over it. Of all my children, my youngest son's going to be the first to get hitched." He frowned at his grown sons, ranging in age from twenty-seven to thirty-one. "What are the rest of you waiting for?"

Gabe, Tanner and Sean's eyes widened and they stared at each other.

Gabe raised a hand. "Now, Dad, don't start."

"Start what?" Jonathon waved a hand around the room. "There are plenty of nice young women around these parts, many of which would be happy to marry into the O'Brien family." Each of his sons stood to inherit large parcels of land when he died. What woman wouldn't want to be a part of that? "You've all proven yourselves good ranchers, increasing the size of our herd, building our stock of working and racing horses. And you've each done good at your other interests. You're all strong and good-looking men, even if I *am* a little biased. 'Course you look like your old man." He puffed out his chest and grinned. "Okay, better, but then I have a few years on you."

"Dad…" Tanner shook his head. "We've been over this. We'll get married."

"Someday," Gabe added.

"When we find the right woman," Sean finished.

A dark-haired beauty passed by, carrying a tray loaded with beer mugs and whiskey shooters. A rowdy cowboy reached out and pinched her ass.

She turned, her cheeks bright pink, and slapped the man in the face, almost spilling the tray of drinks. "Keep your hands to yourself, George."

Jonathon chuckled, liking that she was embarrassed by the unwanted advance, but that she could stand up for herself. She reminded him of his dearly departed wife when she was about that age. "What about her?"

"Isabella?" Gabe asked, his eyes narrowing. "She's pretty, all right. But I've asked and she refuses to go out with me."

"Really?" Sean grinned. "I asked her too, and got the same brush-off."

Tanner's gaze followed Isabella as she wove through the tables. "Apparently, she doesn't care for the O'Briens."

Gabe clapped his brother on the back. "Turned you down too, did she?"

"I didn't say that." Tanner glowered at Gabe.

Jonathon chewed on a toothpick, studying the gal in question. "Got good hips. Would bear children well."

Gabe shook his head. "Dad, we aren't looking for breeding stock."

"She's got nice—" Sean made the universal motion for figure until Tanner planted his elbow in his belly.

"Don't be so coarse." Tanner's brows rose. "Isabella's a nice girl. That's probably why she won't go out with you."

"Did any of you ask her more than once?" Jonathon demanded.

"After she turned me down flat, I didn't see the point." Gabe scratched the five-o'clock shadow on his chin. "Still don't know why she wouldn't even go out for a cup of coffee."

"You were shit-faced drunk. That's why." Tanner lifted his mug and emptied the last swallow. "Point is, Dad, I haven't found the right woman."

"I kinda thought Isabella was that woman. She's not like any of the others." Sean stared after Isabella as she returned to the bar with a tray of empties and orders for more drinks.

"Yeah, she's got a great laugh when you can get her to loosen up." Gabe's gaze followed Isabella as well. "But you can't make someone love you."

"Are any of you even trying to find a woman?" Jonathan glanced at each of his sons, one at a time.

Tanner frowned. "Dad, it's not like shopping. You can't just choose one off the shelf."

"You have to be persistent and let a gal know you're serious." Jonathon smacked his palm on the table. "I want grandchildren. Lots of them. You can't be too picky or all the good ones'll be gone before you know it."

"And how long did it take you to find Mom?" Sean asked.

Jonathon's head rose, his chest swelling. "I fell in love with your mother the first time I saw her. I knew by the second date I was gonna ask her to marry me."

Isabella stopped at their table and collected the empties. When she smiled, all three of Jonathon's sons smiled back. Damned if they weren't taken with this little girl.

"Can I get you boys anything?" she asked.

"Well, as a matter of fact…" Jonathon started.

"Dad…" Gabe warned. "She's asking about drinks."

Jonathon frowned at his oldest son. "I'd like to talk to the owner."

"And we'd like another round." Tanner drew a circle with his finger over the table.

"I'll be back in a minute." Isabella turned, her long, rich, brown hair swinging over her shoulders, and her short, frayed cutoffs barely covering the curve of her ass.

"Yeah, I think she'll do," Jonathon muttered, an idea spinning in his head. "Is Isabella one of the for-hire strippers?"

"I don't think so." Gabe glanced at the dance floor, his boot tapping to the beat of the music. "Why don't you ask her when she comes back?"

"I will." It was about time someone did something about getting his sons married off. Since the three at the table didn't seem to be in any hurry, it was time he took matters in his own hands. "You say a woman owns this place now?" Curious about the owner,

Jonathon craned his neck, searching the interior of the saloon for an older female face that looked like she'd be the owner.

"That's right." Tanner nodded toward the strawberry-blonde beauty behind the bar, helping out. "Audrey Anderson bought it."

"The pretty blonde? Is she old enough to serve whiskey?" Jonathon scratched his head.

Gabe laughed. "She's almost my age, Dad. And she's pretty smart."

"Why don't one of you go out with her?"

"She's taken." Tanner crooked his head toward the tall, dark-skinned Kiowa cowboy leaning on the bar. "Jackson Gray Wolf staked his claim and they seem plenty happy. Wouldn't be surprised to hear wedding bells soon."

"That's what I mean." Jonathon's lips twisted. "If you boys take too long deciding which girl is right for you, you'll miss out on all the good ones."

"Well, hell, Dad, I'd better get out on that dance floor and find me a woman before they get snatched up." Tanner pushed back his chair and stood, cracking his knuckles. "Lemme see. That pretty redhead oughta do." He struck out across the floor for the bar. Before he got there, another man stepped up to the redhead, said something that made her smile and led her out on the dance floor.

Gabe chuckled across the table. "Seems our brother missed his shot at another one of the good ones."

"See what I mean?" Jonathon crossed his arms.

Tanner moved to the brunette who'd been sitting next to the redhead. She shook her head and held up her hand, flashing a wedding ring.

After one more try, Tanner returned to the table, a scowl marring his tanned brow. "Didn't really feel like dancin' anyway. Besides, I think the show is about to start."

Isabella returned with a tray of drinks, plunking them on the wooden tabletop, one at a time.

Jonathon leaned toward her as she passed by him. She even smelled pretty. Yup, if she was willing and the creek didn't rise, he'd hire her to perform at the bachelor party. Maybe that would get the ball rolling.

Audrey Anderson moved in behind Isabella. "I'll take that tray. You'd better get into your costume for the show."

Jonathon's ears perked. "She's in the show?"

"All my girls either sing or dance as part of their duties at the Ugly Stick Saloon." Audrey smiled at Isabella's retreating figure. "And we have a special presentation tonight. A new toy I've added to the Ugly Stick arsenal and hopefully a way for the girls to earn a few more tips." Audrey winked.

"What is it?" Sean leaned forward.

"You'll see." She nodded toward the stage where all three of the Gray Wolf brothers were pushing a big machine out onto the dance floor.

Tanner's frown lightened. "Is that a mechanical bull?"

"Close." Audrey grinned. "It's a mechanical horse. The only one of its kind, as far as I know."

"I've never seen one before. I thought mechanical bulls went out in the seventies." Jonathan had ridden a few mechanical bulls in his younger days. "They never did give the same look and feel of riding the rodeo circuit, but they were good for training and impressing the gals."

"I found this one at an auction and had it repainted and tuned up." She clapped her hands and glanced at the chair beside Jonathon. "Mind if I join you? Isabella is up first and I didn't get to see her practice."

Jonathon jumped up and pulled the chair out for her. "Please. I have something I want to talk to you about after the show."

Audrey dropped into the chair, turning to face the dance floor. "Isabella really didn't want to be the first to perform on the horse in public, but I insisted. She's the best rider we have."

"Why didn't she want to do it?"

"She doesn't think she's sexy enough to pull it off." Audrey snorted. "That girl just needs to look in a mirror."

Jonathon agreed and his sons apparently did too.

Gabe, Sean and Tanner craned their necks, waiting for Isabella to appear.

Jonathon wanted to see Isabella in action as well, before he committed to hiring her for the bachelor party. Although he'd pretty much decided on her anyway. She was pretty, sexy and could take care of herself.

The band struck up the tune to some country song about saving horses and riding cowboys.

From the back of the bar behind the stage, Isabella emerged wearing black leather chaps, black cowboy boots with rhinestone studs and a bright red bikini. Nothing else.

"Hot damn, that outfit makes me horny." Audrey sat forward and hooted along with the rest of the crowd. "Not sexy, my ass. Isabella's hot tonight!"

Isabella's gaze remained fixed on the mechanical horse. She placed her boots one in front of the other as she walked through the throng of cowboys. When she reached the horse, Jackson Gray Wolf grabbed her around the middle and swung her up on the fiberglass body.

"That horse doesn't have a saddle. How's she going to stay on?" Jonathon asked.

"Isabella assured me she was used to riding bareback." Audrey leaned toward Gabe, her eyelids drooping. In a conspiratorial whisper, loud enough for all at the table to hear, she added, "She told me she prefers to ride bareback in the moonlight, but this will have to do."

Jonathon shot a glance at Gabe, Tanner and Sean. Each of his sons' gazes followed the woman up onto the horse, where she straddled the beast, wrapping her legs around its middle. She gave Jackson a nod and he reached to push the On switch.

The horse lurched forward.

Isabella kept her seat, her back straight, her legs tightening around the fiberglass body.

As the music swelled, the horse settled into a smooth and easy rocking motion.

Isabella swayed with the electronic creature, her movements all sex-in-motion.

When the horse spun to the side, she stayed with it, her body twisting and bending in a languid, captivating style.

Jonathon alternated between watching the girl and watching his sons. When the song came to an end, men were tossing twenties at the base of the contraption, yelling for an encore. Gabe rose, his hand going to his pocket. Tanner and Sean followed suit, each reaching for their wallets.

Jonathon grinned. "Yessirree, she's the one."

Smiling broadly, Audrey turned to Jonathon. "I'm sorry, did you say something?"

"Miss Anderson, I have a proposition for you."

She winked, her smile broadening. "Now, Mr. O'Brien, I'll take that as a compliment, however, my man might not." She tossed her hair, motioning toward Jackson who was standing guard beside the mechanical horse and its sin-worthy rider.

"Not that I wouldn't be tempted by such a lovely lady, but I'd like to hire your establishment for my son's bachelor party."

"Now *that* I can do." She turned to face him. "When are you planning this event and what kind of food and entertainment would you like to provide for your guests?"

"A week from today, I'll leave the food up to you,

and I want her." He pointed to the woman on the fake horse. "Is she one of your for-hire strippers?"

Audrey frowned. "No, Isabella made it clear she doesn't want to hire out as a stripper. She doesn't think she's as pretty or sexy as the other girls."

"Seriously?"

"She has confidence issues where her sexuality is concerned. I don't get it, but she does. How about Lacey?" Audrey pointed toward one of the women holding a full tray of beverages, fielding passes from every man at the table she was serving. "Lacey's one of my best and she's sexy as hell."

"Nope." Jonathon nodded toward Isabella and made his stand. "We want her. If you can't get her, the deal's off."

The owner of the Ugly Stick Saloon stared across the floor at Isabella. "She's a beauty, but she's never expressed an interest in stripping." Audrey shrugged. "All I can do is ask."

"Tell her I'll pay her five hundred dollars a dance if she'll do it. And I'll pay you a thousand-dollar commission to get her to agree, on top of renting the saloon for the party." He pulled his wallet out, extracted ten one-hundred-dollar bills and slapped them on the table. "There's a good-faith deposit."

Audrey stared down at the pile of bills. "You don't even know how much I charge to rent the place."

"Money's no problem. I just want that girl there."

"I'll do my best." Audrey picked up the bills and stuffed them into the low-cut top of her shirt inside her red, lace bra just barely visible. "No guarantees. I don't insist on my girls stripping. It's completely up to them."

"I'll be by tomorrow to sign papers."

Audrey leaned back, her brows forming a V over her nose, her lips quirking upward in a smile. "You're a pushy bastard, aren't you?"

"Only way to get what you want."

The woman chuckled. "And I'll bet you get what you want every time."

"That's my aim." He grinned and stuck out his hand. "I'll be by tomorrow. Tell my boys I'll see them at home." He nodded toward his sons, pushing their way through the crowd of men now standing around the horse and its bareback rider, catcalling and hooting with every move of the woman's luscious body. His boys had a thing for this Isabella. Her reluctance to perform as a stripper endeared her to Jonathon even more. She was modest and unassuming about her body. And damned sexy, even if she didn't think so. Even if she wasn't *the one*, she just might get his boys interested in finding a woman and settling down.

Audrey stood, tucking her hands into her back pockets. "Will do, Mr. O'Brien. Drive safely."

His duty done, Jonathon left the Ugly Stick Saloon and headed back to the Rockin' O Ranch, more than determined to see his boys settled.

WHEN THE RAUCOUS cowboy song ended, Isabella had been more than ready to dismount her gallant machine and change into her uniform of cutoff jeans, tank top and cowboy boots. Normally, she wouldn't be caught dead struttin' around in a bikini and cheesy chaps. But when she saw the amount of money the cowboys were throwing on the floor at her feet, she couldn't just walk away. One more song. She could ride for one more song.

Though dancing half-naked in front of a bunch of drunken cowboys wasn't her thing, Isabella had to remind herself that it was all for a good cause. And they didn't seem to mind that she wasn't quite as busty as the other girls, or that she wasn't as graceful and sexy. One of Audrey's requirements of her *girls* was that they either sang or danced in order to get hired on as a waitress at the Ugly Stick Saloon. Since Isabella couldn't carry a tune in a bucket, she'd opted to dance. Not that she'd done much dancin' on the horse ranch. Dancing was like having sex, only in public. And Isabella didn't consider herself sexy.

As liquored up as these men were, anything with a vagina would be sexy to them.

Still, this was her first time performing by herself and she was anything but a performer. Give her a real horse and a decent pair of jeans and she'd show them what real riding was. The sexy outfit was just for show. She hoped it did the trick. Being a sex object had never been one of her goals in life and she wasn't so sure she had all the right equipment to qualify. Her body wasn't shaped like the other girls, and she didn't have the moves. Hell, she was more at home in a barn than in a bedroom. Her track record in relationships had proven that.

Because of her failed love life, she needed this job and the money she could earn through tips. She was saving to buy back Sundance before her ex sold the horse at auction. No amount of tips from waiting tables would add up fast enough to cover the cost of the thoroughbred horse. She needed a way to make big bucks quick. Perhaps this mechanical horse gig would be her ticket.

When the band played a sexy, swaying melody, Isabella motioned for Jackson to switch the horse into a slower, more sensuous action. More capable of holding on with only a light touch, Isabella closed her eyes and imagined herself in another place, a place where she could ride Sundance bareback across lush green fields of hay. The music filled her, dancing and swaying all around, her body moving to the gentle rhythm, her mind entering another dimension, one in which her body ignited and her core heated to molten levels. Wearing nothing but a bikini and chaps, she could imagine all kinds of sexy, naughty things she could do alone with herself or with a man...or men... who knew what it took to please her.

That's where her relationship with her ex-boyfriend, Daniel, had gone wrong. He'd been frustrated and finally insulted that he couldn't get her off. No amount of foreplay on his part brought her to orgasm. Sweet-talk or Daniel's hands sliding across her skin hadn't brought her to that elusive climax she craved, not that Daniel spent a whole lot of time pleasing her. When she didn't come within five minutes of trying, he blamed her and went on about the act of screwing her, calling her frigid and the ice queen.

Isabella's chest constricted. Maybe she was frigid. She'd never considered herself sexy, why should anyone else?

She should have ended their association before it had come to a boiling point. Then maybe Daniel wouldn't have been such a dick about Sundance, the horse she'd raised since he was a gangly colt, all legs and no coordination, her only true friend in this crazy, mixed-up world. He'd been a gift from her father.

Sundance had won his first three races, the long shot, coming out of nowhere, attracting the attention of the Circle C Ranch, who'd made an offer to purchase him.

Isabella had refused to sell, until that fateful day her parents were involved in a tragic automobile accident, killing her father and confining her mother to a hospital bed for several months before she gave up and died. Everything, including their home and property, went to paying off the medical bills and still, it wasn't enough. Isabella had been forced to sell Sundance to the Circle C Ranch. Fortunately, they'd offered her a job caring for him and the other thoroughbreds. That seemed like so long ago. Now she worked at the Ugly Stick Saloon and she hadn't seen Sundance in six months, although she'd followed his track statistics.

Isabella leaned over the mechanical horse's back, pretending to ride like the wind, trying to forget for the moment how much she missed her horse. Someone stuck a riding crop in her hand and she tapped it against her thigh. She'd never used one on Sundance.

A roar of approval rose from the crowd of men, prompting Isabella to open her eyes, reminding her of where she was.

She tapped the crop to her ass and more bills floated to the floor at the base of the imitation horse. *Hmmm. This could be lucrative.* All she had to do was pretend to like a little whip action and the men went wild. Her pussy tightened. Maybe it wasn't all pretending and she wasn't as frigid as Daniel thought.

She arched her back and ran one hand up her side to cup her breast, the other hand rose to lightly tap the crop against her other breast, drawing it across the tip and down the center of her cleavage. The leather against her skin sent heat radiating downward to where her cunt slid across the smooth back of the horse. *This could be addictive.*

"She's so hot, I'm gonna come!" One cowboy cried out, whipping his hat from his head to fan the front of his jeans.

"Keep it in your pants, George. I'm gonna marry that girl." Another cowboy dropped to his knees. "Marry me, Isabella."

Isabella laughed, pressing a hand to her chest, the crop clutched tightly in her fist. Maybe she was going too far with the sexy vamp thing. Maybe she was getting off a little more than she'd intended. Her eyes widened. Hell, she *was* getting off. By herself. Without a man…a miracle as far as her ex was concerned. Her ego took a leap.

"More! We want more!" The men surged forward, jockeying for position at the front of the line.

Jackson Gray Wolf stepped out front, crossing his arms. "Back off!"

"Come on, Jackson, you're blocking the view." A burly man in dusty jeans and a wife-beater shirt lumbered forward. "We wanna see her ride bareback."

Jackson held his ground. "Back up and I'll consider moving. Be a jerk and the show's over."

The men behind the big burly cowboy yelled at him, "Get back, George, we wanna watch."

"Move it, cowboy."

"Let her ride!" A bigger guy than wife-beater-shirt reached out and pulled the obnoxious one out of the way.

Isabella breathed a sigh. One of the O'Brien men. Gabe, she remembered from the time he'd asked her out, shortly after she'd arrived at the Ugly Stick. She'd considered going out with him, but it had been too soon after Daniel dumped her.

At least Gabe wasn't obnoxious like the wife-beater. Still, he looked as hot and bothered as the rest of them, his jeans tight around the groin area. Based on the swell, he had a real boner going there.

Another twinge of excitement nudged at her core. The rocking action of the horse, the feel of leather in her hands and the sight of a handsome aroused man, a gentleman cowboy to boot, all added up to turning her on. Too bad Daniel hadn't figured that out. Then she wouldn't be missing Sundance and wondering when she'd ever see him again. And that was the reason she'd stayed so long with Daniel. The horse. Not the man.

A toothless cowboy surged forward. Jackson cut him off before he reached Isabella.

What would she have done if Jackson hadn't been there to ward off unwanted attention and groping by the drunks in the saloon? Isabella longed for the wide-open spaces of a ranch where she could get away from the crowds.

What she wouldn't give to be doing what she loved the most, working with horses on a large horse ranch. Not that she didn't appreciate all that Audrey had done for her. If it hadn't been for Audrey and the Ugly Stick Saloon, she'd be on the street, flat broke with no way of earning enough money to keep her afloat, much less have any chance in hell of buying her horse from Daniel.

If only she could earn the money faster. She knew that if Daniel couldn't get Sundance to win the next two races, he'd have the horse up on the auction block. Isabella had been the only handler who could work with the horse. The only one who knew how Sundance operated.

The thoroughbred racehorse responded to light nudges, not heavy-handed whipping with a riding crop. Knowing Daniel, he'd gone right to using the crop to get the horse to move. Maybe even out of spite for Isabella's departure. And when Sundance wouldn't respond, Daniel would have blamed Isabella.

Yes, she should have gotten out of that poisonous relationship earlier. She would have, if not for Sundance. Instead, she'd stayed at the Circle C Ranch, working for Daniel and his mother, training and caring for the racehorses until Daniel had fired her as a girlfriend and horse trainer.

Now the closest she'd gotten to a horse was riding the mechanical horse at the Ugly Stick. Which hadn't been as bad as she'd thought it would be. For some strange reason, the rocking motion, the audience of aroused men and the leather crop combined had given her a bigger charge than she'd felt in a long time. Had she been a man, she'd leave the stage with a hard-on. As it was, she felt all warm and wet and ready for anything.

The music ended and Isabella sat for a moment, reining in her lusty thoughts.

Three tall, dark-haired cowboys slid past Jackson and held out their hands to her. Ah, yes, the handsome O'Briens.

Her belly tightened and a rush of heat pooled even lower. Strong, healthy cowboys always held a soft spot in her heart and a hot spot elsewhere. Especially these three. They'd all asked her out at one time. She'd been too freshly rejected by Daniel to even consider dating at the time. And they hadn't asked her again.

"Let me help you down." The oldest, Gabe O'Brien, held out his hands.

She brushed them aside. "I can get down on my

own." Because she was in such a heightened sense of arousal, she couldn't risk letting a man touch her intimately. Not now. Besides, she didn't need a man to help her off a horse, real or mechanical. She slid her leg over the smooth fiberglass body of the horse and dropped to the ground, forgetting it was a little higher than the platform the mechanical horse was attached to.

Tanner, another of the O'Brien men caught her, pulling her against his hard chest to steady her. "Are you okay?"

His breath stirred tendrils of hair near her ear, sending all kinds of shivery shards of electricity bouncing off her skin. "I'm fine." Again, she had to remind herself she didn't need a man in her life. The previous one had ruined her, making her think she didn't have a romantic or erotic bone in her body.

Then why, when Tanner's hands circled her waist, had her body ignited and her breath lodged in her throat?

She'd gone almost six months without a man and Daniel hadn't gotten her as excited during her year-long relationship as the O'Brien men had in less than a second.

Probably because she'd gone six months without any sex. One time with Tanner and she'd be bored and unable to reach that elusive orgasm she'd been longing for, going on a year and a half.

His hands moved lower, curving over her hips. "Would you care to dance?"

"He's got two left cowboy boots." Sean O'Brien

stepped up to Isabella. "Dance with me. I, at least, can do a decent two-step."

Gabe shook his head. "Give the gal some room to breathe, guys." He held out his hand. "She's not interested."

Gabe's commanding voice captured Isabella's attention and without thinking, she put her hand in his.

He extricated her from his brother's arms and led her several steps away. "You make riding bareback an experience that bears watching." Lifting her hand, he turned it over and pressed a kiss to her palm. "Thank you." Then he dropped her hand. "Come on, Tanner, Sean. Leave her alone."

"But, she didn't say no to the dance," Sean argued, his smile turning full-force on Isabella. "Well?"

The younger O'Brien's grin was infectious and Isabella couldn't help returning his smile with a little shake of her head. "Sorry, I have to get back to work."

Tanner lifted his cowboy hat. "Thank you for a great show, ma'am."

With that, the three O'Brien men walked back to their table and sat.

Isabella's brows furrowed as she headed back to the dressing room where she could change into her cutoffs, tank top and cowboy boots, each of the O'Brien men on her mind. All of them as tall as church steeples, broad-shouldered and sun-kissed from working outside. Her dormant sex drive kicked up, reminding her that she was a young female with needs, not a dried-up old biddy. Following on the heels of that thought was the echo of Daniel's parting words. *A man wants to know he can make his woman as hot as she makes him. You bring nothing to that table, lady.*

For the past six months, Isabella had believed that. Bumping into the O'Briens made her think perhaps she wasn't as frigid as Daniel made her out to be. Too bad, she wasn't interested in testing that theory. God forbid Daniel might be right.

Her belly tightened and her pussy throbbed.

Or was she just frightened by the intensity of the heat roiling inside her body at the mere thought of going out with one of the O'Brien men?

# ABOUT THE AUTHOR

Twenty years of livin' and lovin' on a South Texas ranch raising horses, cattle, goats, ostriches and emus left an indelible impression on Myla Jackson, one she likes to instill in her red-hot stories. Myla pens wildly sexy, fun adventures of all genres including historical westerns, medieval tales, romantic suspense, contemporary romance and paranormal beasties of all shapes and sexy sizes. She lives in the tree-covered hills of Northwest Arkansas with her husband of more than 20 years and her muses—the human-wanna-be canines—Chewy and Sweetpea.

*To learn more about Myla Jackson and her alter ego Elle James visit:*

www.mylajackson.com
mylajackson@mylajackson.com